Goodnight
Riley

Goodnight Riley

Lori Johnson

TATE PUBLISHING
AND ENTERPRISES, LLC

Published by Tate Publishing & Enterprises, LLC
127 E. Trade Center Terrace | Mustang, Oklahoma 73064 USA
1.888.361.9473 | www.tatepublishing.com

Tate Publishing is committed to excellence in the publishing industry. The company reflects the philosophy established by the founders, based on Psalm 68:11,
"The Lord gave the word and great was the company of those who published it."

Book design copyright © 2015 by Tate Publishing, LLC. All rights reserved.
Cover design by Carlo Nino Suico
Interior design by Jake Muelle

Published in the United States of America

ISBN: 978-1-62994-143-1
1. Biography & Autobiography / Personal Memoirs
2. Religion / Christian Life / Spiritual Growth
14.11.11

In the golden street of heaven,
As the happy children play
Gentle Jesus watches over them
Caring for them day by day
May you find comfort in knowing
In the Father's home above
Our little one is happy
In the sweetness of His love

Acknowledgements

For my mom, Carole Parks. Although you never were a cheerleader, you always cheered me on to be a better person, a godly woman, and a memory maker. You always believed in me. You have always been my biggest fan. And for that, I want to say thanks! I love you, Mom!

For Taylor "Smiley" Johnson. God knew what He was doing when he gave me a son like you—with your gentle, kind spirit. He knew that when Riley was gone, I would need you, my little buddy. He knew that you would be able to cheer me up with a hug, smile, or card. Though you are not my little three-year-old anymore, you still bring a smile to my face and joy to my heart. I am so proud of the man you have become. I thank God for you and Katie every day. I love you, Tay! PS: Good night, Lois!

For Katie, "Lil' Miss Sunshine." God also knew that I needed a baby girl who would be so full of life and personality, ready to live life in a big way, and ready to share her heart to those who needed to feel loved. You are always able to make people feel special and have brought sunshine to those around you. Your love for God is so incredible and real. I admire that so much. I now have the pleasure of watching you with your own little girl, Selah Grace. What a great mommy you are! I love you to the moon and back!

For Selah Grace Hauck, our first grandbaby. Selah, you are a beautiful blessing from above. You have been prayed for since your mommy and daddy found out they were expecting a baby. The excitement and anticipation was worth all the worry. Selah, I want you to know that no matter what comes your way, you will never be alone. You will always be loved—more than you could ever know. My prayer is that one day you will have a story of your own that will bless those who come into your life. I pray you will be a Christ follower and be a light to those around you. Selah Grace, you have filled my heart, as well as your granddad's ("Pop Pop") heart. I cannot wait to make memories that will last forever! Hugs and kisses from Gramma Gigi.

For my sweet Brian. You are still the man of my dreams, the love of my life, and the man I want to grow old with. Are we at the old part yet? I guess so; after all, we *are* grandparents! Thank you for never wanting to leave when the storms came our way. Thank you for taking the commitment of marriage as forever, together. This year, it will be thirty years we have been married! I am so glad God put us together in the seventh grade. Wow, He really did know what He was doing! I will love you until I take my last breath! Happy thirtieth anniversary, babe!

This is also in loving memory of my dad, Larry Herbert "Poppy" Adams.

I'd like to give a special thanks to Steve Brady Photography for taking pictures at Riley's graveside and Riley's Rock, and also to Tate Publishing for their help in getting our story to the world.

Preface

As I think over all that has happened in my life, I struggle to write. My stomach twists in knots, and I feel sick to my stomach. After twenty-three years, you would think the feeling of anxiety would not be so strong. Reliving the worst day of my life, the worst day of my husband's life, makes the anxiety even stronger. Losing a child is never easy. Reliving it is torture.

Though it is difficult, I must keep reminding myself of the purpose of this book. My hope is that my story will help another grieving soul. If I can help just *one* person, then reliving the pain is worth it.

As you read my story, I pray that you will see how God carried me through and never left my side. Your circumstances may be different, and the loss may not be the same, but our thoughts and emotions are. You are not alone. This book may be hard to read at times, but it is real. And there is hope. I promise that one day, you will smile again. You will laugh again.

1

I grew up in sunny Fort Lauderdale, Florida. I had such a great childhood in a place with beautiful weather and an even more beautiful family. My parents raised me and my brothers in a strong Christian household. I'm so thankful for their diligence in taking us to church. If they hadn't, my life would be so different now.

My mom, Carole, and my dad, Larry, became Christians in 1968. They loved spending time with our family and always let us know we were loved. Dad enjoyed fishing, and we spent many weekends out in the boat on the water. Mom stayed at home with us but was always involved in various civic organizations. They both taught me and my siblings that it was so important to work hard and show love to other people—but most importantly, to love the Lord.

One Sunday morning, my Sunday-school teacher talked about how much God loved us and how He sent His Son, Jesus, to die on the cross for us. I couldn't stop thinking about what the teacher talked about. I was so nervous, but I felt I was ready to ask Jesus into my heart.

When we got home from church, I called my mom into my bedroom and told her what I wanted to do. Mom wanted to make sure I knew what my decision meant. She reminded me this was a free gift from God; it cannot be earned. I asked God to forgive me for my sins, and then I asked Jesus to come into my heart. I will never forget that day. And I never knew how much that childlike faith would one day carry me through the worst time in my life.

When I was seven, my parents announced that we were moving. My dad was a superintendent with Southern Bell, and he was being transferred to Asheville, North Carolina. He wanted a better life for his family. Of course, I was disappointed; my friends were here, and so were my grandparents. If I had only known what was waiting for me, then maybe I wouldn't have protested so much.

When I started seventh grade at AC Reynolds Middle School, my mom was the chairwoman of a Christian woman's club. She had met a young woman named Jean, whose younger brother, Brian, attended the same school. Mom was afraid I would miss my friends from the school I had previously attended. Jean made sure her brother found me. It's because of those women that my life changed forever.

One day, while I was in class, a friend of Brian's threw a folded note on my desk. It was from Brian. I was so nervous: my first note from a boy! When I unfolded the note, I read: "Will you go with me? Check yes or no."

I checked no at first, but shortly thereafter, I changed my mind. Brian was always so sweet. We dated off and on; it's difficult to be in a relationship when you're too young to drive! We would talk on the phone sometimes and stayed on friendly terms.

When we were freshmen, though, we got back together. We would meet in the library and sometimes get caught sharing a kiss. The librarian, Ethel "Jake" Jacobson, seemed to always keep her eyes peeled for the cheerleader and football player spending too much time in the biography section. Jake knew we were pretty good kids, and she would write us an excused note sometimes if we were going to be late for class. Jake was awesome! Brian and I were inseparable! He was at my house all the time. If he heard it was going to snow, he would hurry over to my house so he could get snowed in with me! My parents never caught on! I don't think it would've mattered; they loved Brian too.

I still feel bad that I was not always as kind to him during those times. I broke up with him a few times, but he never broke up with me. He never said anything bad about me when I was dating someone else and being a brat. The way he treated me when we were apart was one of the reasons I loved him; he loved me no matter how I acted. I had to kiss a few frogs, but in the end, I realized I had my prince all along beside me!

If I didn't know it then, I knew it when I read his note to me in my senior book:

> Well, Lori, what can I say to my baby doll? Thanks so much for making my senior year the best year ever for me. You know how I feel about ACR. I love it, but there is a time to continue life. Who knows where we'll be in two or three short years? No one knows, but I do know that we will be together. It's really gonna be sad leaving, but I'll always look forward to what's ahead for us, and I'm looking forward to that special day when our dream finally comes true. You've left some great memories in my head, about the times at Reynolds. You know we've had a lot. I could go on and on forever, but I am going to save some things for the annual. You'll never know how much you mean to me. Thank you for a very special senior year.
>
> I love you,
> Brian
> 1 Corinthians 13: 4–8

As our senior year of high school started to wind down, Brian and I knew we had to start planning for our futures. The questions were numerous: Would we go to college? A trade school? Would we just get jobs? We weren't sure. The only thing we were sure of was that we didn't want to be separated.

In the end, I decided to attend cosmetology school followed by the Vidal Sassoon Academy. Brian went to the University of North Carolina at Asheville to major in business.

In 1984, just a year after high school graduation, I became Mrs. Brian Johnson! As newlyweds, we had a lot of growing up to do. When we came home from our honeymoon, we realized we were late on our first house payment. We had purchased a fixer-upper and, unfortunately, finances were something that took us a long time to understand. We were always a day late and a dollar short. What we didn't have monetarily, we made up for in love.

I loved being Mrs. Brian Johnson—still do, as a matter of fact! In those first days of our marriage, I tried so hard to be Super Wife. I worked full time at a salon but always made sure to keep the house clean, Brian's clothes ironed, and dinner on the table.

We talked about starting our family, but we knew that we wanted to wait until Brian was finished with college.

2

One morning, after Brian went off to work, I was eating breakfast and went to take my birth control. I picked up my little pink container and gasped. I had missed a pill last week! I started to panic. Surely, missing *one* pill wouldn't be enough for me to get pregnant, right? I didn't think anything about it…until later that day.

I left for the salon and went about my day. During my lunch break, I started feeling a little queasy. The missed pill popped into my head. I left early and picked up an EPT (early pregnancy test) on the way home.

I was so nervous. My parents and I were in the middle of remodeling an old house to turn into a hair salon. I think I was more nervous about telling them than I was Brian! They had both worked so hard to help me; I just didn't want them to be upset.

When I got home, I took the test. Sure enough, three minutes after taking the test, a little pink plus sign appeared. I made the first available appointment with my doctor. Once he confirmed my suspicions, I drove to UPS where Brian was working and told him the big news. "Well…I guess we're having a baby! Ready or not!"

We weren't sure if we were having a boy or a girl, and we wanted it to be a surprise. So much to the annoyance of our friends and family, we chose to wait until the big day to find out if the nursery would be pink or blue.

As my belly grew, my Super Wife mentality started to shrink. The cooking and cleaning became a little harder. Ironing came to a halt. Brian's uniforms were sometimes so wrinkled he was asked if he was wearing a road map! I felt bad for him, but my body just couldn't keep up with the way things were done a few months earlier.

Cutting hair became harder the bigger I got; you can only get so close to a client when you have a growing belly. Being pregnant was hard at times, but I loved it! It felt amazing to know that I was growing a little blessing that was part me, part Brian.

We could not wait to see our baby. We wanted to know what he or she looked like, his or her personality...We just couldn't wait! I think our little bundle was anxious to see us too, as he arrived five weeks early.

Brian Taylor Johnson was born on June 15, 1987. Because he was born premature, Taylor was rushed to the neonatal nursery. He was having trouble breathing, and at thirty-six weeks, his lungs were not fully developed. He was struggling to survive, and we were struggling to stay strong. We leaned on one another and our relationships with the Lord to get us through.

The neonatal nursery became our home for the next five weeks. Taylor was so fragile at this stage, I was not allowed to hold him. I couldn't hold my newborn son. My heart ached as I sat by his incubator; just looking at him made me cry. He was on oxygen and had wires coming out of his little body. He also had to be fed through a feeding tube. His little feet were always so blue.

Even though it wasn't ideal, the doctors and nurses we had were amazing! They knew how hard it was for us to see our baby like this and were very understanding. We hated leaving Taylor at night but knew we could call the neonatal unit at any time of the day. They were always happy to give me an update—even at 3:00 a.m.

Our parents were a huge support during this time as well. They stayed right by our side during this scary ordeal. And they prayed without ceasing.

Brian and I prayed more during this time than we had ever before. Our faith was being tested for sure. Even though I was worried, I knew Taylor was going to be all right. He just had to be! I trusted that God would heal Taylor—and He did!

Taylor was released from the hospital after five long weeks. When he was discharged, his doctor said he was perfectly healthy and did not expect any long-term problems. Taylor was not only a miracle but a true gift from God.

Shortly after I had Taylor, I dreamed I was having twins. When I told Brian, he laughed and went on with his day. I also shared my dream with my mom and a friend, and we all laughed at what that would be like and how hard that would be. I never gave the dream a second thought.

Fast forward three years later to 1989. One morning, I woke up not feeling right. I was nauseous, and I felt physically drained. I thought I might be pregnant but wasn't quite sure. I gave my doctor a call and made an appointment. My doctor wanted to see me.

"So how are you feeling?" my doctor asked.

"I feel a little worse than I did when I was pregnant with Taylor," I said. "Maybe I just have the flu?"

"Let's go ahead and do an ultrasound," the doctor said after pressing on my stomach, "just to make sure everything's okay."

I started to get nervous. My blood work wasn't even back yet. Why would he want to do an ultrasound? My hands shook as I laid back and pulled up my shirt.

The nurse squirted the gel and rubbed it on my stomach. She was very focused and had a look of stern concentration. I was trying to read her expression. Suddenly, I saw her smile.

"Well, looks like we've got a bit of a problem," she said. "This right here is Baby A"—she pointed to the screen—"and this is Baby B."

"Wait, what?" I said, in shock.

"Lori, you're having twins!" the nurse exclaimed.

I started smiling and laughing with excitement. My dream was a premonition after all! The nurse said she had never seen someone so happy to find out they were having twins. Usually, they are just in shock!

I cannot even begin to describe how I felt. No one in our family has ever had twins. Mom and her doctor thought she was having twins when she was pregnant with my brother, Larry (she even had a baby shower for twins!). During her pregnancy, she hemorrhaged so much she thought she had miscarried. She ended up delivering only one baby. She will always believe she had been carrying twins. How could someone not believe in God? Look what He can do!

I could not wait to tell Brian and our parents. The drive home seemed to take forever! I was hitting every red light, and it was as if every slow driver in town was getting in front of me. I was practically bouncing in my seat; the anticipation was killing me!

When I finally pulled in our driveway, Brian was already home from work. He came out to the car to greet me when he saw me pull up. He saw the look of excitement on my face but mistook it to mean something was wrong.

"What's wrong? What did the doctor say?"

"He did, actually," I said. "He…said we're having twins!"

Brian started laughing. "No he didn't," he said, smiling. I nodded. "He did!"

"Seriously?"

"Yes, seriously!"

He wrapped his arms around me and gave me a big hug. Then he reminded me of my dream a few years earlier I had totally forgotten! I took the ultrasound pictures out of my purse and showed them to Brian. I pointed out Baby A and Baby B. The smile on his face was unforgettable; he was just taking it all in. Behind his smile, I could tell his mind was already going with so many worries and thoughts about how we would care for these little angels. Even so, I knew it would all be okay.

When I called my mom, she didn't believe me either. It took a little convincing, but when she finally realized I was being truthful, she was excited. But, as a mom, she was also worried. Taylor was five weeks early, so I was already considered high risk. Now I was carrying *two* babies. I was 5'2" and weighed 110 pounds; this was going to be a snug fit!

My belly started growing very fast. Taylor was so confused as to why Mommy's body was changing so quickly. I bought a book about becoming a big brother and read it to Taylor—a lot! He knew how special his role was and was very excited.

Because I was carrying twins, I would get tired so quickly. Cleaning and laundry took a back seat, and I felt a little guilty. Brian was so supportive, though. He was a huge help with Taylor and even offered his back for a resting place for my legs at night so I could get comfortable and get a little sleep.

After several months of pregnancy, I became sick with bronchitis. I could not stop coughing; my ribs hurt from coughing so much. I went to see my doctor for a checkup, and he let me know the twins were coming sooner than we expected. The coughing was actually putting pressure on the babies! I was put on bed rest and could only get up to shower or use the bathroom. That was very hard to do with a two-year-old!

Thankfully, my mom came to the rescue and suggested we move in with her and Dad. Their beautiful house quickly became a day care. My parents built the greatest play area for Taylor under the basement steps. Mom had her work cut out for her. Taylor was sweet but a very busy little boy. Add his two-year-old buddies, and I know Mom felt as though she was running a day care.

My friends were also a huge help during this time. They would take Taylor for a few hours so Mom could get a break. But when they brought him home, they would stay and visit while the toddlers ran around the house. I was a constant nervous wreck!

Anytime there was a mess, I felt awful that my mother had to be the one to clean it up. One day, a friend of mine stopped by with cupcakes topped with blue icing. The icing must have been two inches high! I could see right away this was not a good idea. Taylor's little buddies crammed down their cupcakes and ran off to play. When I looked in the kitchen, I saw Mom's expensive rug covered with drop-pings of blue icing! I waddled into the kitchen and started to clean—only to be busted by Mom. She sent me back to the couch and cleaned it herself.

My mom and dad took over most of the care and discipline of Taylor, which meant he had Gramma and Poppy wrapped around his little finger. He was the little king, since he was the only grandchild on my side of the family. I told them that Taylor needed naps, even though he did not like them.

My mom would take him to a room upstairs for his naps. As soon as Mom was back downstairs after putting him in bed, we would hear the pitter-patter of little feet. We would yell upstairs for him to get back in bed. He could never figure out how we knew he was up! After many failed attempts, he would finally give up and fall asleep. And as soon as he would wake up (with his sweaty curls and red cheeks), he would want to snuggle. I loved that part of the day!

3

Christmas had come and gone, and it was now the middle of January. The twins were due in a little over a month, and I was feeling miserable. My ankles were swollen, my back ached, and I couldn't even walk to the bathroom without huffing and puffing.

One day, I started in on one of my coughing fits. And when I coughed really hard, I knew something had happened. I felt like I was going to pop. These two babies wanted out! Mom drove me to the hospital, and Brian's parents went to get him from work.

When we got checked in at the hospital, I immediately asked for my epidural. I was beyond ready to get some relief. But, as luck would have it, the shot only worked on one side. I was still in pain and couldn't even fathom how I was going to deliver twins naturally with only part of my body numb.

The nurse, thankfully, came to my rescue! She tilted my bed sideways, and in seconds, I was completely numb. I felt like I could finally relax. While we waited for the on-call doctor to finish his lunch break, Brian and I had fun joking around and were excited to finally get to see our babies. I was still very nervous about delivering these little bundles five weeks early, but as Brian and I laughed, I felt a sense of peace come over me.

When the doctor arrived, he checked to see how dilated I was. After he checked me, he exclaimed, "Let's do this!"

"Wait, what?" I asked, looking at him.

"It's time," he said and smiled. "You can do this, Lori. You and these babies are going to be fine."

Brian kissed my forehead and held my hand. I nodded to him and said, "Okay, I'm ready."

Katlyn "Katie" Louise Johnson was the first to arrive. She was perfect in every way, a beautiful baby. After a few more pushes, I did it all over again. Riley Scott Johnson was not used to being alone in my belly, and he was ready to follow his sister into this world. I just could not believe these two miracles. If I didn't believe in God before now, I would have surely believed! How can people not believe in God after seeing the birth of a baby?

I looked up at Brian and saw a tear running down his cheek. He leaned in and gave me a kiss on the cheek. I knew he was wondering how in the world I just did that! I am sure he was so proud of me.

After I held the babies, they were taken out of the room to be checked. While Katie was ready for the world, the second she popped out, Riley stopped breathing a few seconds at birth. He was taken straight to the neonatal nursery. The doctor told me everything looked good, but they just wanted to be 100 percent sure.

They brought Katie to my recovery room and said I could feed her. The nurse came in with the bottle of formula prepared and handed my little Katie to me. She did so well with the bottle! As I fed her, I asked the nurse how Riley was doing. She went to get the doctor who told me that he wanted Riley to stay in the neonatal nursery until he could drink from his bottle without struggling.

Two days later, Brian and I were allowed to take Katie home. I was excited and heartbroken at the same time. I wanted my twins to go home together. Poor Riley was still not drinking his bottle like he needed to and still needed to gain some weight before they allowed him to come home.

When we got home, Taylor was so confused when he saw us with just one baby, when he had heard us talk about *two* babies. Life was insane. I was juggling Katie and Taylor and Brian was working two jobs. He would go to the hospital to see Riley on his lunch break and after work. Mom was helping me and spending time at the hospital. My dad never left the hospital. Dad and Riley quickly developed a special bond.

Riley stayed in the neonatal nursery for about two weeks. When he was finally able to leave the hospital, I was thrilled! We were all finally going to be together! When we asked Taylor who we were going to get, he answered, "Kadee!" We would explain that we were picking up Riley. Taylor thought he had two Katies.

We stayed with my parents for a few weeks after the twins were born. But we finally moved back into our two-bedroom bungalow. Home sweet home!

When Riley came home, my days were nonstop. They were filled with bottles, diapers, baths, laundry, and keeping up with Taylor. He loved his "two Katies." My mom would come over in the mornings during the week to help with the twins. She loved giving them their baths, and that became their special time. This also allowed me to have Taylor and Mommy time and get Taylor ready for the day.

The feeding schedule was tough. I had to keep up with which baby ate first. Riley took his time drinking his bottle, and Katie downed hers in seconds. In no time at all, the twins were chubby and a healthy weight. They were so cuddly and adorable!

Keeping up with a toddler and two babies fewer than three years old was a challenge. When they were all taking a nap, I would hurry to do laundry, make bottles, and clean up—just so I could sit down for five minutes. I was exhausted! But there is no rest for the weary. We were constantly having people drop in. I loved to visit, but I would pay for it. After a while, I decided to hang the "Baby Sleeping" sign from the nursery on my front door to let our friends know we were all napping and now was not a good visiting time. So many times, I would go to the front door and find diapers, presents, formula, and containers of cookies. Some of the gifts were from people we didn't even know! I was amazed to see gifts from people I knew were struggling to make ends meet. People just wanted to help— and it was so appreciated! I loved my crazy, busy life!

Taylor adapted so well to being a big brother. He was so proud of the twins. When family and friends stopped by, he would show them off. People would bring him a present when they came to see the twins. And Taylor quickly learned how to feed one of the babies just like I was. He was such a big boy! One of my biggest worries was that Taylor would feel left out. I don't think he ever had a problem with that. I think he knew how much people loved him.

From early on, Katie knew she had to compete with her brothers for Mommy's special one-on-one time. When I would reach into the crib to get Katie, she was all smiles. When I would reach in to get Riley, she would quickly turn her smile into a full-blown cry. I could not believe it! As soon as I laid Riley down and picked Katie up, she would smile again. What a stinker! Katie wanted to be held all the time, and Riley was content to patiently wait his turn.

Riley never cried. Anytime I needed to leave the house, I would take Riley because he was always so happy and content. He went with the flow. I would leave Brian home with the other two while Riley and I went out for our one-on-one time. I was worried Riley would feel left out. Katie, with her bubbly personality and big hair bows, always stopped a crowd. And Taylor was our first born. I had to make sure Riley was shown the attention he needed as well.

When I think back to these times, it puts a smile on my face. These were some of our best memories. It was all about being with the people you love. Was our life chaotic? Yes. Was it worth it? Oh, yes. It is sometimes the smallest things in life that are the most special. As hard as it was, it worked for us. We were committed to our family. Once you make that commitment, you never look back.

One day, we had visitors all day. It seemed like everyone we knew stopped by to see Taylor and the twins—the grandparents, close friends, and even a special client of mine. That night, Brian and I collapsed into bed talking about how blessed we were. Our lives were wonderful, and our kids were a joy! Taylor was the cake, and the twins were the icing. We laughed and kissed good-night. I went to sleep happy, thankful, and blessed. I will never forget that night.

The next morning, I went to check on the kids. Taylor was asleep in his bed, and Katie was in her swing sound asleep. Riley was asleep in his portable crib. Sometimes, we had to put Katie in her swing to sleep because she would keep Riley awake if they were in the bed together. Katie was always ready to play!

Normally, I would get Riley up first so I could have some quality time with him. I had to take special moments to give Riley his one-on-one Mommy time. As I was reaching to pick Riley up, I noticed a purple dot on his arm that I had never seen before. I didn't think it was anything until I noticed Riley lying on his stomach. My heart started to pound, and I felt like time was slowing down. My hands shook as I reached to pick him up. As I pulled him out of his crib, he was limp; he was purple and his nose was flat.

I hardly remember what happened next. All I remember is screaming and crying. Somehow, I made it to the phone to call 911.

"I think my baby is dead!" I screamed, over and over. They told me they would send someone soon.

I called my mom. As soon as she picked up the phone, she knew something was wrong.

"It's Riley!" I cried. "I think he is dead!"

Unbeknownst to me, my neighbor heard me screaming and let herself in to comfort me. Taylor just kept staring at me, and I know he was so scared. There was nothing I could do. I was so helpless! Everything happened so fast!

The ambulance arrived and took Riley. Mom and Dad came and took me to the hospital. I knew that if Riley was going to be a vegetable or hooked up to machines for the rest of his life, I did not want that. It would be so hard for him to see his sister doing things he would never be able to do. He just looked so awful, and I knew there was no way he would be right again. I pray that one day I can get that picture of what Riley looked like out of my mind.

I am not sure who called Brian's parents, but they went to Brian at work and told him he needed to go to the hospital and that something had happened to Riley. I cannot imagine the horror Brian had to be going through. The unknown is always so scary.

We all sat in the waiting room, silent and scared. So many thoughts were running through my mind. *Why did this have to happen to Riley? Did I do something wrong? Is he going to be okay? Can we get through this?*

After what felt like forever, the doctor came out. When I saw her eyes well up with tears, I knew what she was going to say.

"I am so sorry," she said, her voice breaking. "There was nothing we could do."

Brian and I held each other and wept. When we finally went in to say good-bye to our little angel, Brian, Taylor and I stood and looked at him. He looked so beautiful and perfect, like he was sleeping. I did not want to leave him. I couldn't leave him. I couldn't believe he was gone forever. We left, completely in shock.

When the autopsy came back, it showed that Riley had died from Sudden Infant Death Syndrome (SIDS). He was almost six months old. We always talked about how we felt Riley was an angel. He never cried, was always sweet, and never made a fuss. God made him special because *He* knew. He knew Riley would only live a short time, so He made sure we had plenty of one-on-one time with our little guy. That was God's plan all along. I am so thankful for those special precious moments. They were such a blessing.

4

Everything happened so fast. One night, we were putting a healthy, happy baby boy to bed. Now we were at a funeral home, planning his memorial. Brian and I did not want to do this. We did not want to be here. We wanted to be home, with our three children. But we couldn't.

As I followed the funeral director into a room, my stomach sank and stifled a sob. It never crossed my mind there would be such little caskets. And it never crossed my mind I would need to pick one out. This wasn't fair! Why did we have to be here? Why did our little boy, so sweet and innocent, have to be taken from us? My mind was reeling. I couldn't look at the small caskets anymore. I distracted myself by looking at something, anything besides them.

I spotted a clock on the wall. I stared at it for a moment. I felt an overwhelming sense of peace rush over me. I started to feel strength renewed within me. I knew I could do this. I felt God there with me, helping me through this moment. I had never felt His presence like that before.

After we picked out the casket and left, Brian and I got in the car.

"Did you notice the clock in that room?" he asked me. I nodded.

"This may sound weird," he said slowly. "But...when I looked at it...I just felt *peace*. Just like, a huge rush of it."

I felt my eyes well with tears. "I did too," I said, reaching for his hand.

Brian leaned over and kissed my cheek. God was definitely helping us through this, even if we didn't know why it happened.

A few days later, Brian and I were at the store and saw a lady we knew. She came up to us and told us she was sorry for our loss. She said as soon as she heard the news, she dropped what she was doing and prayed.

"It was Tuesday, around two o'clock in the afternoon," she said.

Brian and I thanked her. We gave each other a small, knowing smile. That was the exact time and date that we were picking out Riley's casket. God used that sweet lady to show us that He is real—today and always.

When I sat down to write Riley's obituary, it solidified to me that he wasn't coming back. I don't think it had really set in until that moment. It was simple, but it was all I could write:

> Riley Scott Johnson, infant son of Brian and Lori Adams Johnson of 6 Kensington Drive, Beverly Hills, died Thursday in a local hospital.
>
> Surviving, in addition to his parents, are a brother, Taylor Johnson; a sister, Katlyn Johnson; maternal grandparents, Mr. and Mrs. Larry Adams of Asheville; paternal grandparents, Mr. and Mrs. Hal Johnson of Asheville; maternal great-grandparents, Mr. and Mrs. Clifford Adams of Fort Lauderdale; and paternal great-grandmother, Margaret Horner, of Roxboro, North Carolina.
>
> Private graveside services will be at 10:30 a.m. Saturday in Calvary Episcopal Church yard. Memorial services will be at 11:00 a.m. Saturday at

Arden Presbyterian Church. The Rev. Ed Graham
will officiate.
Williams Funeral Services will announce
arrangements.

After Riley's funeral, we went to my mother's house. We
had cried until we had no more tears. Taylor said something that was so adorable; I can't remember what it was.
All I know is, it made us laugh! I think God gives children
to us to help with the healing—and to bring laughter right
when we need it. At first, I felt bad for laughing on such a
somber day. But then I realized laughter is acceptable, and
needed, to move forward.

A few days after we laid Riley to rest, a friend of mine
came to visit. She brought me a journal. It was yellow with
flowers on it, and it even had a little lock—like a child's
diary. She thought it might help me to write out my feelings, thoughts, and fears as I grieved.

I didn't know if it would help me or not. I had never
kept a diary as a girl, and I didn't even have the focus to
write a grocery list right now, let alone a journal entry. I
took it and thanked her.

I woke up in the middle of the night that night, unable
to go back to sleep. I couldn't stop thinking about Riley.
I went to the kitchen to pour a glass of milk and saw the
journal sitting on the counter. I decided to open it up and
write. From then on, I wrote in it as much as possible.

June 20, 1990, 1:30 a.m.

I don't really know who I'm writing this to, but I
just want to express the way I'm feeling. I guess this
seems like the only way. I miss Riley so much. He
was so special to me, just like Katie and Taylor are.

I know Katie Bug misses him so bad. When she sees another baby, she gets so alert. It's almost like she's trying to get close to them as if it were Riley. She sometimes moans, and it's something she didn't do until Riley died.

I still can't believe he's not with us. I feel so incomplete. I know I won't feel complete until the day comes when I see my baby again.

Taylor asks about him. It's so hard because he really loved him so much. He never really got jealous. We have Riley's picture in our den. The other day, Taylor said, "Oh, what cute hair!" as he pointed to the picture. He's also "fed" the picture of Riley with a spoon. I want Taylor to always remember Riley.

It's really hard sometimes to see his picture because I miss him so much. I can't believe how this has changed my life. I am so afraid to leave Taylor and Katie. I don't ever want to lose them. I want to be the best mom ever. I hope Brian and I can be open about Riley's death. Brian is so afraid to talk about Riley because he doesn't want to upset me. I want him to talk about Riley. He was our little guy. I was so excited about having twins that I felt doubly blessed.

I wouldn't want this to happen to someone else, but it sure is hard when it happens to you. I am glad I have a true God. I don't know what I'd do if I would never see Riley again. A lot of good things have happened because of Riley. I know God took Riley for a reason, but I miss him so much. I trust that God will get me through this awful time.

Today, I went shopping, and I saw some cute boy clothes, and I thought for a split second that I could buy something for Riley. I just got the sickest feeling when I realized he's really gone. It's so crazy how attached you get to a baby. He had so much character, even at almost six months. He laughed all the time. I think the only time he cried was when he was hungry. You could make him laugh so easily. I miss that more than anything.

I loved watching him and Katie in the bed beside each other. They were just starting to really respond to one another. Riley always tried to touch Katie. He always would quit crying when we would lay her next to him. I loved dressing them alike. They looked so cute.

I was so proud to have three beautiful babies. I often said it's too good to be true. I'll never say that again. It's so weird how even when I don't think I'm thinking about Riley, deep down inside, I am. I haven't been back to the cemetery because it's too painful. I hope Riley knows how much I miss him. Everyone does. The grandparents, aunts, uncles, everyone.

Brian and I are going away this weekend. It will be hard leaving Taylor and Katie. I think Brian and I need to have some alone time.

June 23, 1990

Today is mine and Brian's anniversary.

I miss Riley so much, and journaling seems to be the only way to feel better. I was so afraid I would forget the details of Riley over time. I hope one day, I can share this book with Katie and Taylor to share reminders of our little Riley.

A few nights ago, I could not sleep. I missed Riley so much. He was so special to me, and we all miss him so much. When Katie sees another baby, her little face lights up. It's like she is looking for her brother. I don't know what I would do without a terrific husband and kids. I want Katie and Taylor to grow to be close. They need each other. Someone once told me twins have a kind of mystical bond. It's something no one else can understand. Another friend told me a twin never feels the same if one dies. Riley and Katie slept in the same crib. They sucked each other's thumb! Once I walked in and Katie was holding Riley's ear. It was such a comfort to know the other was right there. It was so precious and I smile just thinking about it. I miss those moments. I know Katie misses that as well. I am sure her crib feels so empty. She has started whimpering—not quite a cry, but a whimper. My mom noticed the whimpering as well. I think it's her way of telling us that something is missing.

June 28, 1990

I cannot believe Riley has been gone for three weeks. I've had some rough days, but God gets me through. Yesterday, Riley's birth certificate came in the mail. It had his footprints on the back. It was so unexpected. I was so unprepared. I wanted to scream. I went to my bedroom to escape the house full of people. I tried to crawl out of my bedroom window, but the freshly painted window was stuck shut. I just needed to go away and scream out loud. I was always surrounded by people, and I needed to be alone. I needed to let my feelings out. I couldn't stop crying.

I asked God to reveal Himself to me. I tested Him by demanding that He help me through this.

All of my life, I had believed in God, but now that Riley was gone, it felt like He was not there for me.

I cried myself to sleep clinging to a picture of Riley. I wanted to grab him out of the picture. I sometimes just sit and stare at that picture. It's all I have left of him.

God hears our cry. Isaiah 30:19 says, "You shall weep no more. He will be very gracious to you at the sound of your cry. When He hears it, He will answer your cry."

Our entire family has the flu. Today was Katie's first doctor's appointment since Riley died. And, of course, I see a lady with twins in the doctor's office. They looked poor, and the mother was yelling at them. The mother looked like she led a hard life. I wondered if she was as excited to have twins as I had been. At this moment, I realized I could become bitter. I had to make a conscious decision how I would be.

5

I was so blessed to have almost six months with both Riley and Katie, together as twins should be. My friends couldn't believe my energy, and they could not imagine how I managed three small children. I was beyond grateful to have them with me during such a difficult time. Taylor was my little buddy and loved to dote on Katie. He would bring books to her and read them. He could make her laugh like no one else.

As time went on, I was hopeful to make new memories, especially in our new home that we bought just after the twins arrived. From the first time we saw this house, we knew it was perfect. There was a bedroom we thought would be perfect for Taylor and Riley to share—a large room with a small dormer room connected to it, perfect for two boys. That was the plan Brian and I had. It just wasn't God's plan. He knew Riley's future and was preparing a room for him in heaven.

Brian asked me once if he thought Riley was growing up in heaven or if he'd stay the same. I wondered the same thing. I didn't want to miss anything of his growing up, and I feel like I did. I am sure when I get to heaven, we will have lots of catching up to do. I cannot wait!

A few weeks after Riley's funeral, I went to the mailbox. Normally, I would receive at least three cards in the mail.

That day, there were none. My heart ached, not because I felt like people weren't thinking of us or praying for us, but that it showed that the loss wasn't new anymore—that time was passing by.

I knew it had to be that way; you can't stop time. But it hurt just the same. I looked forward to those special cards and sweet words of encouragement. Life is so tough at times, but those cards helped me through. I now fully understand what it means to have a broken heart. It is a real feeling. It really hurts.

When the cards stopped, I picked up my journal more. I'd write in it whenever I was feeling particularly sad. It was cathartic to see my pain written on the pages of that book. Putting those words and thoughts on paper somehow released me of the tension, anger, sorrow, and bitterness I was carrying.

July 2, 1990

Today, Mom said that when she thinks of Riley, she thinks of his smile. It's so true. It is so hard not to think of him with us because he was so happy all of the time. He had such a rough start in the hospital. But I am so thankful I had almost six months with him. Before he died, I told Mom that he was like a little angel—always smiling and never crying.

I love my husband so much. I would have never found him on my own. God definitely helped by bringing us together. God knew the man I would need for what my future held. Brian is lying next to me sound asleep. I can't sleep.

Tomorrow, I have aerobics. I always loved taking the kids, and it is hard to go back. Taylor goes to the nursery, and I will bring Katie in to class with me. She and Riley used to sit there and just stare at us ladies dancing around. I am sure we were pretty funny to watch! My friend Susan is picking us up. She says that if I am not dressed when she gets here, she will dress me and put me in her car. I was not quite ready to face what used to be a happy place. It's now so hard to go to. But I am thankful she has given me that push. My kids need that. I needed that. Such a special group of sweet ladies. Aerobics followed by a devotion and prayer time. I need this. I have to do this to move forward. Or, at least, try.

July 4, 1990

This is the first holiday without Riley. We are all going to Mom and Dad's for a cookout. I was supposed to host but was not feeling up to it. We made cupcakes with flags on top. Taylor is excited. Katie and Taylor are asleep, Brian is washing the car, and I am lying in the sun. It's nice to have a few relaxing moments.

We went out for dinner the other night, and the waiter gave Taylor a balloon. That night, we gathered in the front yard and let the balloon go to Riley. This is something Taylor can do to make Riley happy. From now on, balloons go to heaven. The next day, Aunt Jean asked Taylor where the balloon went. With a big smile, Taylor said it went to see Riley.

It is so important to me that Katie and Taylor talk about Riley. He is part of them, too. He will always be a part of us and we realize the importance of talking about him. If we were to stuff our feelings and memories of him deep down inside, we are never able to heal. It's also important to let the kids know that if something were to happen to them, we would never forget them, either. I don't get it when people push pictures and memories aside when someone dies. It is hard to see pictures of Riley, but it is important to deal with our hurt head on. With time, this will get easier. Hour by hour. Day by day. Week by week.

Taylor talks about Riley at least once a day, and he will not let Katie out of his sight. If we go anywhere, Taylor wants Katie to go too. I have gotten so overprotective since Riley died, and I do not want either of the kids out of my sight. I have so much fear of something happening to them.

Psalm 56:3 says, "Whenever I am afraid, I will trust in you."

While Taylor is napping in his bed, he has been sleeping in our bed at night. This is something we said we would never make a habit of, but we are both okay with it for now. Taylor and I saw Riley being loaded into the ambulance, and I am afraid this is having quite an effect on him. I pray he does not remember how his little brother looked that day. I know, eventually, he will have to go back to his own bed, but that will be so hard. I feel so secure having him next to me.

I check on Katie so many times while she is sleeping. Her room is upstairs in our house, but I feel better having her close to us as well. I would have her in our bed, too, if she wasn't so small. We spoke to Dr. Parks, her pediatrician, about putting Katie on a monitor while she was sleeping. He seemed to think that, since she is older now, the monitor would constantly beep, and then we would worry the beeping meant she was not breathing. We cannot live with that. We have had enough fear.

I cannot believe how fast time has gone by. It has almost been a month since Riley died. I always thought that when I died, I would be united with my parents and grandparents in heaven. I never imagined my child would be there waiting for me. It is so hard to believe that my baby has gone to heaven before me. I never imagined I would not see each of my children grow and have families of their own. I wonder what they will look like when they are older. I cannot wait for Taylor to play baseball and for Katie to dance. I pray they will be polite, confident, and have the love of God like Brian and I do. I pray that Katie and Taylor accept Jesus into their hearts so we can all be in heaven together. I will make sure I do my part to teach them about the love of God. I pray that whatever my children do, they succeed. I always want to encourage them and never discourage them.

Taylor has just woken up and has a dirty diaper. Taylor is so loving and gives me hugs and kisses all the time. Yesterday, Aunt Jean told Taylor the two of them were buddies. He quickly let her know that his mommy is his buddy. I hope we will always be! I hate getting mad at him. It hurts me. He hates hearing the word no. I guess he doesn't hear it often enough. We will be playing in his baby pool after I change his stinky diaper. Oh my!

Riley, I will be thinking of you all through the day.

I can't understand why this happened to us. I cannot pray right now, but I feel God is close to me. I can't explain it, but I know God has His arms around me and my family.

I love you, Riley.

July 6, 1990

Today is Brian's birthday; he's twenty-five. It seems weird not having Riley.

I had an okay day. Katie was in such a great mood tonight and jabbered all night! Taylor did not want to go to bed—as usual. We heard stomping upstairs, so I sent Brian up. He found Taylor running around in his diaper and cowboy boots! Such a cutie!

I went to aerobics today. The girls are so great. They continue to pray for our family and that we find comfort and continue to be strengthened. This group of incredible ladies has become my support group. My friends are great and are always asking how I am. I never want to stop talking about Riley. In some ways, I feel that by talking about him, a part of him is still here.

I think losing a child has to be the worst thing a family can go through. I know God is the great comforter. I also know it is only God that is getting Brian and me through this. I know He knows how I feel because He saw His son, Jesus, suffer and die— and it was all for us. I cannot see the big picture of Riley's death, but maybe one day, I will. Maybe one day, I will understand. It is hard to imagine Riley lived such a short life. I read something that gives me comfort: "Your little one served its purpose. A brief life is not an incomplete life." This is so true. God knew what was in store for Riley. He knew what was best. Riley could have suffered from a life of illness or brain damage or a lingering, incurable disease. God knew all of this, and I can now be certain about Riley's future. I love him so much that I have to believe God knows best. It still hurts. Will it always hurt?

I miss you, little Riley.

I am also comforted by 2 Corinthians 1:3–4: Blessed be the God and Father of our Lord Jesus Christ, the Father of mercies and God of all comfort, who comforts us in all our tribulations, that we may be able to comfort those who are in any trouble, with the comfort which we ourselves have been given by God.

"The Great Shepherd of the sheep, the Lord Jesus Christ our Savior, has reached into His flock and has picked up your lamb. He did not do this to rob you, but to lead you out and upward." I have never wanted to go to heaven as much as I do now. I miss Riley, but I have realized I still have so much to take care of here on earth first.

I need to be a good mom and raise Katie and Taylor to have a love for God. My prayer right now is that my children will get saved. God, please let them see your love for them. I love you, God, and I thank you for watching over Riley even though it hurts me so much. Please help me not to be a bitter person; that would be using Riley's life in a negative way. It would not be good for my husband or kids. Help me to use this tragedy in my life for good, and let me help someone else.

Good night, Riley.

Well…it's still July 6, and I don't want to close my eyes. I looked up and saw Riley's picture, and his sweet face just kills me. His hair was just starting to come in. He had one dimple and was the fattest, cutest baby. I loved his cuddly ways, his big blue eyes, and his never ending smiles. I will never forget him looking at me from his crib. He would bob his head up and down when he was waking from his naps. As soon as he saw me, he would give me a big smile. I miss giving Riley his bath. He loved his bath. I loved rubbing his little head with his fuzzy hair.

I think back on the struggle he had the first three weeks of his life. All of the neonatal nurses loved holding him. He was just so chubby and cuddly. We hated having him separated from Katie. I even stayed an extra day in the hospital hoping Riley would be able to go home with us. After being inside my belly together for so long, I know the twins hated being apart. I know Katie is hating being apart from Riley now.

July 8, 1990

Oh, Lord, when will it get better? I miss him so much. I hate turning out the lights. It makes me want Riley even more. There are so many questions with no answers. I think that is what makes it so hard at times.

July 12, 1990

Today, I really missed Riley. Thursdays are the hardest.

I talked to Mom about the day Riley died. I think it's good for me to think back to that day. I am able to talk about the thing that has hurt me the most.

Katie never wants to lie down. As soon as I put her in her swing, she falls asleep. But she quickly wakes up and cries. I pick her up and all is fine. She is spoiled rotten!

On Tuesday, Sarah and JP Branham brought us a beautiful plum tree in memory of Riley. They are so thoughtful. We planted the tree in the front yard. So many friends have given us flowers to plant. Whenever our tree or our flowers bloom, we will be reminded of Riley growing in heaven.

6

July 15, 1990

Taylor had Bible School this week. He really loves it. I helped on Tuesday, and again today. The kids are so cute! I have got to get Taylor potty-trained. He is one of two in his class who is still in diapers.

I have had a busy week! I helped with Bible School, and we had a sleepover. Taylor's friend, Kelli, spent the night. She is so adorable! I curled her hair and painted her fingernails. Taylor did not like sharing me with someone else; they even fought over who would sit next to me. It is good to be busy. It keeps my mind from wandering too much.

Kelli's sister, Maggie, is close to Katie's age. When we put them on a blanket together, my heart aches. Seeing Katie next to a little baby who's the same age as her, as Riley, it reminds me that he's not here. It is so hard not having him here. I think of Riley without even realizing it. I cannot believe he is gone.

Will I feel happy again? Will I laugh or smile again? I am so sad that I cannot ever see myself happy again—at least not like I was before. But I have to keep going. I have Katie and Taylor to think about. I have to give them what they need. And I need to be there for Brian. I know he must feel completely helpless at times. I cannot think of being with him intimately because I am not there mentally.

We went to church today for the first time since Riley died. Katie looked so precious in a bonnet Mom bought her. She looked just like a doll. After church, we went to an Italian restaurant. Last time we were here, Riley was with us.

I think one of the hardest things about losing a child is the first of everything: the first time at church without that child, the first time at a restaurant without that child, the first holidays, buckling the kids in the van and realizing you are missing one. Sometimes, going through my day, my grief hits me hard. It hurts deep inside. I call those moments "Riley Moments." A day filled with moments is a "Riley Day." My friends understand that I do not want to talk or explain what I am sad about if it is a Riley Day.

The last few days, Katie has been wearing some of her outfits that matched some we had for Riley. We had so many matching outfits for the two of them. I know I should go through his clothes, but I just can't do it yet. I just want to hold onto his things for now.

I've had a lot of alone time lately. It has been really good. My girlfriends think I will want more kids. I don't think so. I would be so scared something would happen. Plus, Brian had the "clip-clip" after we had the twins. We knew three little ones would keep us on our toes. We didn't know what was to come. I wish now he hadn't had the procedure. But if we have another one, would it be for the right reasons? Would we be trying to fill a void that can never be filled?

We drove by the hospital the other day. Taylor said, "Mommy was there!" That was both the happiest and the saddest place for Brian and me. I was so happy to give birth to our three children there but so sad to say good-bye to our little guy there. And, once again, I was brought back to our memories of Riley's birth.

I spent every day at the neonatal nursery. The nurses loved to hold him. He was so sweet and was always smiling—no matter the circumstances. I remember how he liked to scrunch down in his blanket. I think the lights hurt his little eyes.

There is not a day that goes by that Taylor does not ask about Riley. Two nights ago, we were lying in his bed, and I told him how much I loved to cuddle with him. He mentioned Riley, and I told him Riley was probably cuddling with Jesus. Imagine being tucked in by Jesus! Taylor got the biggest smile on his face. It is so great that kids can be comforted by such simple words.

Taylor has asked many times to go see Riley. I tell him one day we will all get to see Riley. I told him that Riley lives in heaven with Jesus. We have talked about heaven and how great it will be. I told him heaven is better than his favorite toy and better than anything on this earth. No more tears. No more pain.

Dad is coming over tomorrow to work in our kitchen. Mom is coming over to paint. I love when they come over. And I love to see them with Katie and Taylor. I don't think they could ever get too much of their grandparents. I love seeing them make memories.

I am so sleepy!

Good night, Riley! I love and miss you.

July 22, 1990

It's been awhile since I have written in my journal. I think that is a good thing. I have been so busy with Katie and Taylor.

I sold some of Taylor's clothes at the flea market. I was hoping to pass these down to Riley, but instead, I will use the money to get our couch covered.

Today, someone asked Brian how the twins were. He said it felt like he was hit with a ton of bricks. You feel terrible—and so does the person asking. No one really knows what to say. Some of the sweetest words are the ones left unspoken. You know what the person wants to say but can't. No words seem right. A smile or a hug seems to say it all and means so much.

Katie is finally starting to get some hair. She has been rolling all over the place and is so social. She doesn't like to lie down and even falls asleep sitting up. I cannot believe she is seven months old! I just love this age! We took Katie with us to Diane and Jerry's house last night. Diane gave me a few blankets for Katie to sleep with in the playpen while we visited. I am weird about blankets. I only like for her to have one. I know this has to do with Riley, and I hope to get over this.

Taylor is getting sweeter by the day. He always says, "I love you, Mommies." It makes me feel great. I love it when he shakes Brian's hand and says, "Always buddies!" He is still potty training… Oh what fun! He is so stubborn! I hope he will get the hang of it soon. He cannot go to college with diapers!

Brian is such a great dad. I hope Katie and Taylor realize how crazy he is about them. He always wants to be at home with us—or wants to take us wherever he goes.

This week, I have been wondering what Riley would be doing. Would he be rolling over yet? Probably not since he was so pudgy. I would love to see him in the walker. Katie loves it, and I wonder if he would have liked it too. I wonder if he has a lot of hair, and I wonder how much he has grown. I wonder how he and Katie would react to each other. My wondering will probably never stop.

I've got to go to bed. I love you, Riley.

Sometime in July

It's 11:36 p.m.

I talked to Mom today, and she always makes me feel so much better. I have been a bear to live with and be around.

I saw a video of Riley last night. It was so cute. It is so hard to see Riley and Katie together. He really adored her. He was the one always reaching for her. He would watch every move she made. And he slept so well with Katie by his side. I loved when they slept in the wicker bassinet. I clearly remember the first night feeding two babies. Brian fed one while I fed the other. Riley was a slow feeder at first, but after a while, he would finish Katie's bottle as well! He really did become pudgy overnight. In the beginning, he needed to gain weight, and he had finally started to look healthy.

I think back on all of the gifts people brought us: two of everything and always a little something for

Taylor. It is weird to look at Riley's pictures. I still cannot believe he is gone.

I have not really been "here" lately. All I want to do is think of Riley. I don't want to neglect my responsibilities as a mom and a wife, but it is so hard sometimes. I have a hard time coping with everyday activities when my insides are hurting so bad. I am realizing Riley will never come back. I try not to cry in front of Taylor. It is so frustrating; I cannot seem to do anything. I can usually make things better or fix what is broken. This situation is completely out of my hands. This will never be over. That's why it hurts so much. At times, I feel so alone. I know I never am. I know I am not the only one that hurts.

Brian also hurts. He holds so much inside. I wish I could just read his mind. I want him to open up to me, but he doesn't. It is so hard. I keep thinking he doesn't have much to say. I know everyone deals with death in their own way. It is so important to deal with and not block it out.

Mom and Dad are grieving too. Mom has had a few bad days lately. I know they're trying to be strong for me. I think it's hitting them all at once. They feel like they need to be strong for me because I have two children to take care of. Dad was always with Riley when he stayed in the hospital after he was born. They had a special bond. Dad tears up every time we talk about Riley. They are such special people. They hurt for me as I hurt. I am so grateful for the two of them during my pregnancy with the twins. I have no clue how they took care of very pregnant me, Brian, and Taylor. They did everything for us.

Riley would have loved our new home. Sometimes I wonder if something was wrong with him that we did not know about. It wouldn't have mattered. I would have loved him the same.

Mom is coming over tomorrow. I need to go to sleep. I don't want to be a grump.

Good night, Riley!

7

July 31, 1990

Today has been an okay day. I worked out and then came home to lie out in the sun. I was supposed to go to the pool, but there were going to be a lot of kids' camps there. That is just too crowded for me. I missed Riley a lot today. Sometimes it is hard to journal because sometimes it makes me sad. I don't want to be sad. I want to be up for Brian, Katie, and Taylor.

Last night, we went to a friend's house, and it was nice. They lost a child, Kelly, several years ago. They help us so much because they have been through the same thing. It is crazy how little things can hurt the most. Carol was telling me Kelly loved catching fireflies. When her son started catching them, all she could think about was her daughter doing the same thing just days before she died. It hurts to see others so sad. She showed me a picture of Kelly, and I just cried. For the first time, I knew what it was like for our friends to come to our house and see pictures of Riley.

Carol's husband, Tim, sent this sweet letter to Brian on June 19, 1990; shortly after Riley died, I folded it up and placed it in this journal. I wanted to keep it. It was so sweet:

Dear Brian,

Although we haven't met, I've felt a need to write to you and express my sorrow to you and Lori. I'm sure that Lori has mentioned my wife, Carol, to you and the loss we experienced with the death of our daughter, Kelly, three years ago.

We have been concerned for you and Lori, and we are so sorry that you are now facing a tragedy. As a father who has been through the death of his child, I can imagine the struggles you may now be facing. For weeks after Kelly died, I felt I had no other men to share my hurt, confusion, and disappointment with. It seemed as though I was facing a very lonely and painful future.

But with time, I did have the opportunity to talk with other fathers who had experienced similar tragedies. And sharing with others helped me to better cope with an overpowering situation.

I just want you to know that if the time comes when you feel a need to talk with another father, I would welcome hearing from you. While I certainly don't have answers, I do share a common experience with you, and I would be glad to help in any way I can.

Tim Harrison

The letter Tim wrote to Brian meant so much. It is so hard for men to open up to other men or to show emotion. I'm so thankful that he reached out to Brian.

Taylor's potty training is going okay. While we were at the Harrison's last night, I thought Taylor had a stinky diaper. When I went to check, I realized I had not actually put a diaper on him at all! It's hard to keep up with underwear and diapers when you're dealing with so much. It's a wonder I'm able to get myself dressed in the morning and the kids fed.

Katie slept through the night last night for the first time. I woke up at 6:30 a.m. in a panic. Why had she not woken up? I wanted to go check on her; I was so scared something had happened. But I was afraid to go get her...afraid of what I would find. But I had to.

My hand shook as I turned the knob on her door. I walked timidly to her crib. When I looked down at her, that cute little girl was sleeping so peacefully. Thank you, God. I am trying so hard not to worry and put Katie and Taylor in your hands. I wonder if Brian worries like I do.

Brian and I took Katie and Taylor to Cherokee. Taylor loved it. We just had to get away from home. We are always getting unexpected company, and I was not up for that. Brian knows just what I need. He is such a great husband, and I pray we are always this close. I don't know what I would do without him. I love him so much.

A friend came over the other day, and we wondered if Riley was listening to us talk. I know deep down that he is not, but it makes me want to be a better person—just in case. God can see everything. God is such a great God. He sees everything in everyone's life, the good and the bad, and that must hurt Him. He loves us no matter what we do. He never leaves us. And because of that, I want to be a better person.

Tomorrow, Mom and Dad leave for Mom's class reunion. I will be so glad when they get back. I cannot imagine not having them here anymore. I pray they live very long lives. I feel so safe when they are around. I want them to be here to see Katie and Taylor grow up. Taylor has so many memories with them already—his first garden at Poppy's, his Sesame Street playroom, looking for golf balls, Easter, Santa. Every day should be a memory; memories are what we hold so close to our hearts. Life is a memory—both good and bad.

Riley was a good memory. I thank God for giving me those memories of my little Riley. Good night, Riley. I love you!

August 1, 1990

Another beginning of another month. I cannot believe summer is almost over. Today, I went to Wicker Mart, and they have Halloween decorations out already! That is entirely too early.

Dad called, and he and Mom are in St. Augustine, Florida. Mom is really sick. Dad thinks she ate bad shrimp. Yuck! I hope she feels better before the reunion.

Today was a little depressing. I went through Riley's clothes, and I still cannot believe he is not coming back. I will never see him in these adorable clothes. I picked up a pair of Oshkosh overalls and tried to picture what he would look like in them. Katie has a matching pair. I remember imagining a picture of the two of them in their overalls. I always pictured him being a lot bigger than Katie.

I want him back. I want to know what Riley is doing. I want to know what he looks like with his hair coming in. I bet he looks just like Brian. I sometimes called him my little Brian.

I also found Riley's Precious Moments story-book. I wish I could read it to him. He also loved the stuffed bear Mom bought him. He would start smiling as soon as I put it in his crib. I found his Bible from Bill and Mary Dot. I hope to give it to Katie when she gets married; I want her to have something of Riley's on her wedding day. I hope she feels close to Riley when she is old enough to understand. I also found Riley's winter "bear suit"; it's this fuzzy little sleeper that keeps babies warm while they're outside in the cold. Katie had a matching white suit. They looked so cute in their bear suits with just their eyes peering out. While in a store, a lady thought I was holding a stuffed animal!

I started to remember all of the places we took Riley. I don't want to forget anything about him, and I am afraid I will. This is why this journal is so important to me.

I remember taking Riley to a fundraiser at AC Reynolds High School. I had to cheer, so the whole family came along. I was so proud of my family. Granny watched Riley while he slept in his car seat. I just had to wake him up so all of my friends could meet the twins.

I started thinking back to my pregnancy today. It was hard from the start. But I was not even a worrier until Taylor was in the neonatal nursery. Because of that, so many people prayed for us when I was pregnant with the twins. I just wanted my babies to be okay. God answered that prayer and gave us beautiful healthy twins.

Shopping with three was an experience. Taylor in the shopping cart, Riley in the infant seat, and Katie in the carrier attached to me. Some of the comments made me laugh: "Oh! You're the one with twins!" "How do you do it?" "Are they identical?" "They're not all yours, are they?" I just smiled. This was normal to me. It was fun. I am sure people wondered if I knew what caused so many kids. I did!

The first time Brian and I went to dinner with all three kids, we looked pretty funny. This kid-friendly restaurant would be perfect. Oh, were we wrong! What was I thinking? Brian had to wait in line to order, while I stayed with the three kids. I was a nervous wreck. Taylor acted up, Katie screamed, and Riley decided he would wake up. People started staring. I would never let Brian leave me alone with all three in a public place again! When we were leaving, we made a plan: Brian carried one twin, I carry the other, and Taylor held onto Brian's pants leg. These plans never work! Taylor wanted to be held too. Brian would put Taylor on his shoulders, dodging everything overhead. We'd just laugh.

I knew it was tough for Taylor to adjust to life with the twins. Before the twins, I would take Taylor with me everywhere I went. He went to footballs games and on weekend trips. He was a great baby and adjusted to whatever schedule we had him on. He is so sweet and lovable. Everyone loves him so much. He always tells me how much he loves me ("as big as the golf course!").

He sings all the time. His favorite song at the moment is "Jesus Loves Me." He loves to help Brian and me with whatever we're doing. But when we try to help him, it's a different story. He is very independent and wants to do everything by himself. He loves to walk the golf course with Brian and me. He loves making roads out of masking tape. He loves swinging on a tree swing in Grandma and Poppy's

yard. He loves helping Paw-Paw work on the car—
and especially loves it when they wash the car!

Taylor brightens my day every single morning.
He also loves Katie and loves taking care of her. She
adores him too!

It's almost football season, and I am so glad! I'm
ready to root for AC Reynolds! It will be a great
distraction for all of us.

I am so tired! Good night Riley, Katie, and
Taylor. I love you!

8

August 2, 1990

A friend gave me a bookmark today that said, "God, grant me the serenity to accept the things I cannot change, courage to change the things I can, and the wisdom to know the difference."

I like that.

I've been trying to find verses that will give me some encouragement as I go throughout my day. I've tried memorizing them so I can recite them out loud or in my head whenever I started feeling depressed. Maybe I should just write them down so I can turn to them quickly.

Romans 15:13 (NIV): "May the God of hope fill you with joy and peace as you trust in Him, so that you may overflow with hope by the power of the Holy Spirit."

First Thessalonians 4:13–14: And now, dear brothers and sisters, we want you to know what will happen to the believers who have died so that you may not grieve like people who have no hope. For since we believe that Jesus died and rose to life again, we also believe that when Jesus returns, God will bring back with Him the believers who have died.

Psalms 18:30: As for God, His way is perfect. The word of the Lord is flawless. He is a shield for all who take refuge in Him.

John 14:1–4: Do not let your hearts be troubled. Trust in God; trust also in me. In my Father's house are many rooms; if not, I would have told you. I am going to prepare a place for you. I will come back and take you to be with me that you may also be where I am.

Psalms 62:5–6: Find rest, oh, my soul, in God alone. My hope comes from Him. He alone is my rock and my salvation. He is my fortress. I shall not be shaken.

Psalm 34:18: The Lord is near to the broken-hearted and saves those who are crushed in spirit.

Matthew 19:14: Jesus said, "Let the little children come to me and do not hinder them, for the kingdom of heaven belongs to such as these."

Second Corinthians 4:17–18 (NLT): "For our present troubles are small and won't last very long. Yet they produce for us a glory that vastly outweighs them and will last forever! So we don't look at the troubles we can see now; rather, we fix our gaze on things that cannot be seen. For the things we see now will soon be gone, but the things we cannot see will last forever."

Romans 12:15: Be happy with those who are happy. Weep with those who weep.

Matthew 6:19 (NLT): "Don't store up treasures here on earth, where moths eat them and rust destroys them, and where thieves break in and steal."

Money, things, stuff, big house, trips, etc. Could any of these things bring Riley back? No. None of that helps us in the storms and trials of life. The only thing that can get us through is faith in Christ.

It comforts and gives us peace. I truly feel God walking with me every day. Did I want to give up? Yes. But, somehow, God keeps me moving forward.

God, thank you for these words from You to help me get through this hard time. It is by Your grace that I am able to get through this hard time. Please, oh, God, help me to have a happy day tomorrow. Thursdays are always so awful.

August 23, 1990

I haven't written in a while. I miss Riley so much.

We went to Diane and Jerry's house for their son, Michael's birthday. One of Mom's friends gave the twins matching sailor suits with hats. Katie's was white with pink stripes, and Riley's was white with navy stripes. I did not want to get rid of Riley's suit but knew if I gave it to anyone, it would be Diane, my best friend since seventh grade. Michael could wear it. It felt good to give it to her.

It has been a gloomy day. Yesterday, Mom painted Noah's Ark on the kids' playroom wall. Mom talked a lot about Riley. I know my parents really miss him. It makes me feel like I am not alone in my grief. Sometimes, I feel like everyone has forgotten Riley—even though I know they haven't. I think people don't want to bring him up because they think I will get sad. A recent devotion at aerobics class was about God as our Rock. It is mentioned so many times in the Bible. God is my Rock when I am weak and cannot be strong.

Lately, when I think of Riley, I get sick to my stomach. I have got to think of something besides Riley. I can't help it; I miss him so much! I wish I could see what he is doing.

Katie is getting so close to me. While in her walker, she will go through the house looking for me—room by room until she finds me. When she sees me, she lights up with a big smile. She wants to be right at my feet. I love it!

Taylor is in a new stage in life. He has gotten really private about his potty training. He jumps up and says he is going to be private. If I try to interfere, he says, "Mommy, get out!"

He will be a great husband one day. He always compliments me and notices if I do my hair, wear earrings, or have on perfume. Maybe he sees Brian noticing those things. He starts school in two weeks! I hope he likes his new school as much as he did the old one. I have heard such great things about this school, and it is close to our house. I will miss my little buddy.

Football season is almost here, and Reynolds plays Friday night. I hope Brian will be home from work in time to go to the game.

Tonight, I have made dinner reservations at Steak-n-Ale. Mary is babysitting for us. I hope Brian is not too tired when he gets home. He is such a hard worker and works such long hours. I just want us to be able to talk without interruptions. I hope he will open up about Riley. I hope he knows how much I appreciate him. I am so busy with the kids, laundry, cooking, cleaning, changing diapers, potty training, snack time, nap time, and play time. Then it starts over the next day. Sometimes, I am so busy that I forget to let him know how much I appreciate all he does for our family. Sometimes, I am just trying to stay above water!

My Uncle Harry wrote Mom a letter and told her about tears in the Bible. When a woman lost a loved one to death, she would put a tear bottle under her eye to catch her tears. The tear bottles would be placed with the person who died. I never knew that! The Bible says that tears count as part of our body. That makes me happy. I'm not sure why, but it does.

When we were saying good-bye to Riley, I knew I had to let him go. I just didn't want to. I knew I would not see him for a long time. He looked perfect in his casket. Before they closed his casket, I placed my tear filled Kleenex next to Riley. It held my tears, and I felt like part of me would be with him. I had no clue this was something women did in the Bible. Once again, God has given me comfort.

The funeral home we chose for Riley was close to our house. I could not sleep that night thinking of Riley being so close. I kept thinking I did not want him to be alone. I know that when he died, he went to be with Jesus, but I could not stop thinking of him in the casket. I wanted to see him one last time—but I couldn't.

First Thessalonians 4:13: For since we believe that Jesus died and rose to life again, we also believe that when Jesus returns, God will bring back with Him the believers who have died.

I have got to keep remembering that verse. As soon as Riley died, he opened his eyes in heaven. This is my hope!

August 31, 1990

It has been a while since I have written anything. I have been so busy.

I gave a friend of mine a baby shower. That's been taking up a lot of my time. I didn't think it would bother me, but halfway through the shower, I started thinking of Riley. Everyone was talking about their babies, and I felt I was leaving out Riley. I know he isn't feeling left out. It's just me letting my mind run away. I miss him so much! I know he and Katie would have been so close now.

Our sweet friend, Cecily watched Katie the other day. She is crazy about my kids. When I go to Bible study, she watches Katie for me. When Taylor and I picked up Katie, Taylor said, "Cecily misses her friend." I asked Taylor who he was talking about. "Her little friend is Riley." It just about killed me. Taylor is so sweet. I look at him, and I get so scared that God will take him—or Katie. I cannot even begin to think about that. When I have those awful thoughts, I immediately ask God to take away that fear. He does!

We went to church on Sunday. Mom told me many people said I looked pretty. When she said that, she teared up. She said this was the first time she has seen a sparkle in my eyes since Riley died. I never thought that I looked different. Before Riley died, I was always smiling and having fun every day. I was spontaneous and loved being silly and joking around. Having three kids under three was hard at times, but it was well worth it. I had so much to be thankful for. I guess that all stopped. I didn't think about that until Mom mentioned it. I love my mom. I am going to be okay.

Katie is growing so fast. She is curious about everything. I wish she had her little brother. She has a little fuzz on her head but is pretty much still bald. A cute baldy! Dr. Parks thinks she will be petite.

Taylor starts preschool on Wednesday. I will miss him so much. He is my buddy during the day.

I know he will be fine. It's me I am worried about. He has show and tell on the first day; they really get them involved early!

I am starting a jazz class on Wednesday with my best friend, Diane. Anything we do together is fun. I am getting excited about it. It will be fun, and it will be nice to think about something other than the last few months. I am still going to exercise class. It is the highlight of my week.

I really love our new home. It is really coming along. Mom puts a lot of special touches in our house. If we were not constantly working on the house, I would stay depressed. Fixing it up really helps me put my mind on something other than Riley. I wish I had more memories of him in this house, but the ones I have will always be close to my heart.

It's also nice to have Mom around to talk to. I hope she realizes how much she is helping me—and more than just on the house. I will miss our talks when she is gone. I don't even want to think about the day she is not here for me to talk to. Dad is really helping a lot too. And Taylor likes helping him.

Brian and I haven't talked about Riley much lately. I think we are trying not to be sad. Today, I thought about what Riley would look like. I will probably do that forever.

Sometimes, I get upset when I think of Riley. I take it out on everyone. I just get grouchy—and I hate that! I don't want to be that way. I need to work on that. I know others are hurting too. We were truly blessed by Riley's life. I do not know how people go through the loss of a child without God. They have no hope, and I could not live without hope.

Taylor is waiting for me to tuck him in. We always ask God to be with Riley.

Riley, we will never forget your smile, dimple, fat feet, beautiful blue eyes, brown fuzzy hair, and that sweet spirit that you had. Good night, Riley! I love you!

Tomorrow starts Labor Day weekend. The holidays always bother me. I don't have much else to say tonight except that I would give anything to see what Riley is doing right now. I hope my grandmother is taking care of him. I was so special to her, so I am sure Riley has become special to her as well.

September 5, 1990

Riley, I miss you. I miss you. I miss you. I love you. I love you. I love you. I miss you. I love you. I have wanted to say that every day since you have been gone. I have never meant the words "I miss you" or "I love you" like I mean them now.

God, please let me know in some way that I will see Riley again. I know I will, but I just need to keep my eyes on you. Please keep me by your side. I need you now more than ever.

Today was Taylor's first day of preschool. He was adorable. It broke my heart when I left him at his new school. He wore his new Reebok tennis shoes, blue jeans, and a Nike shirt. He is growing up so fast!

I started my jazz class today, and it was so much fun! Diane and I laughed the whole time. It felt so good to laugh.

Good night, Riley!

September 9, 1990

It's Sunday, and that means a visit to Mom and Dad's for football and chili. A sure sign that fall is on its way.

While flipping through my Bible, I came across a page to record births and deaths in the family. I have never paid attention to that page before. I cannot write down Riley's name. I just stared at the page. I still cannot believe he is gone.

My friend Susan called today to tell me her mom is having some tests run. She has three knots on her head, and the doctors are concerned. Our friend, Joan's mother died of cancer of the brain, so Susan is asking us all for prayers. Susan is so scared. I felt so bad. We have to think positively and place her mom in God's hands.

September 10, 1990

Today I felt blah and kind of depressed. Nothing specific happened.

Katie has been really fussy. She is so spoiled! I love her so much, and it is so hard to let her cry.

When I went to get Taylor from school, his teacher let me know he had an accident. Taylor told the teacher she needed to go buy him new underwear since he was not going to put the messy ones back on. It took forever for him to get potty trained, but now that he was he was not going to put on dirty under-wear! I love it! I now carry an extra pair with me.

It looks like a storm is coming. I am disappointed, because I wanted to leave Brian a note to meet us at the park for a picnic. I thought a picnic might help buoy my spirits. But my plans got rained out.

Brian seems to be doing okay. He hasn't said much about Riley lately, but I know he thinks about him. Brian asked me if I liked his job. I don't like the long hours, but I do not want to complain. He doesn't need any more pressure than what he is already under. I told him if I won Publisher's Clearinghouse Sweepstakes, he can quit his job, ha!

My aerobics class is great! A few days ago, we were sharing something we were thankful for. I said I was thankful for this group of incredible ladies. I started crying because they prayed for me when I couldn't pray for myself. They have said so many prayers for me and my family. They hurt with me, and they shared with me struggles they have been through. This group of ladies will never know how much they mean to me. They help me get up in the mornings. I look forward to our exercise, prayer, and devotion. I hope one day, I will be able to show them the love they have given me.

When I was leaving class, someone said, "I love you, Lori." Those words were so sweet to hear that I started crying. Today's tears were those of thanksgiving and love for the women in this group.

Mom is also great! She is always here for me and always doing things to pick me up. She took me to the Carpenter Shop to look for a book about dealing with grief over the loss of a child. She then took me and the kids to the fair. Taylor loved it, and Katie screamed from excitement. My mom is so great; she knows me inside and out and knows when I need help and is always there to help. I love her!

Today was a "Riley Day," and I put on a tape Mom gave me with Bill Gaither singing. I wanted to hear "Because He Lives." Because He lives, I can face tomorrow!

We found out why Katie was being so fussy. She was having back-to-back ear infections. I felt so bad for her. Dr. Parks sent her to an ear, nose, and throat specialist.

Mom and Taylor came with us to the appointment. While we were waiting for the doctor, Katie started acting differently. She felt hot and seemed lethargic. We asked the nurse to have the doctor come in, but she let us know he would be there shortly. After a few minutes of waiting, Katie started foaming at the mouth. I could not help but think of Riley, and I started to panic. Mom started to panic too. She said, "Let's go!"

We decided to leave the specialist's office and rushed down the road to our pediatrician's office. We have never moved so fast! I could not believe what was happening. Taylor was scared.

As soon as we got to the pediatrician's office, one of the doctors saw us and said, "Bring her back! She has lost one child, and we will not let her lose another!" They did a spinal tap and called 911.

Katie was rushed to the hospital. She was having a seizure as a result of her temperature spiking. She did not recognize me and was unresponsive. This was so scary!

Taylor saw the gurney and asked, "Gramma, is my baby sister going to die?" Mom was taken back. I cannot imagine how that hurt her heart. Taylor is so thoughtful, and that breaks my heart. He was so scared for his little sister. Katie was his buddy.

Katie was home in just a few days. The doctor said we should not have to worry about this again. I cannot even begin to imagine losing her too.

God, please keep my children safe.

9

September 11, 1990

We are headed to Fontana Village for a getaway. My brother and his girlfriend are riding with us; I hope they don't mind two little ones! We planned this trip before Riley died, and I cannot stop thinking how he should be here with us. I brought a picture of Riley, Katie, and Taylor to the lake with us. It makes me feel like Riley is here.

I want to have a good time on this trip. I know I will think of Riley, but I do not want to be sad. I don't want to put a damper on everyone's fun. I am determined to have a good time.

It's now 11:00 p.m., and it has been a very busy day. We have had so much fun. We played Pictionary and went out in the boat. Taylor is exhausted, and I pray he is in a good mood tomorrow. Katie slept the whole time in the boat. I feel like I have escaped from reality.

As the day wound down and the kids were getting ready for bed, I started to feel guilty. Why was I having so much fun? I shouldn't be allowed to have fun anymore. How could I be happy, knowing that part of our family isn't here? Riley should be here. He should be here, laughing and cooing with his siblings, watching me smile. Can he see me smiling and enjoying myself? Is he disappointed in me? Does he think I've forgotten?

Riley, I love you. I wish you were here, but I know you have plenty of people who are happy you are with them in heaven. I think of you all the time. You are always on my mind and forever in my heart. I love you.

God, please keep us all safe.

September 14, 1990

We are leaving Fontana. Taylor is ready to be home. Katie is crying. This will be a fun ride home!

Our stay at the lake was perfect. We spent most of the time on the boat. I was even able to nap! Granny and Paw-Paw were such a big help and let Brian and I have some special time alone with Taylor while they watched Katie. Taylor loved the lake and the boat. I was so scared he would not like the water. Brian and I went waterskiing. Brian was able to drop a ski, but I was happy with my two skis.

I am sure I gained weight while we were away. We ate so much junk food. I cannot wait to get back to normal food at home.

I didn't write in my journal every day like I thought I would. I didn't want to get sad thinking of Riley. It was good for me to have a break. When Riley died, it was all I could do to get through my day. Minute by minute, hour by hour. I feel as though now, I am able to go from week to week. I don't cry as much. I have some days I don't cry. But I have some days, I think of Riley, and I cannot stop crying. But I must remain strong and be there for my family.

A friend of mine recently asked if I felt bitter about Riley's death. I said I didn't think so. I guess I could easily become bitter. I had to make a choice when Riley died to either be angry and bitter because of this tragedy or try to be the best wife and mom I could be. Riley would not want me to be bitter and take his death out on Katie, Taylor, or Brian. I do not want that. It is so hard to keep going, but I have to—for my family. They need me. And I am so glad they do. I am finally able to accept help from others. I am so thankful for the family and friends that have not given up on me. I know it was hard for them too.

I try to imagine what heaven is like. I have driven myself crazy trying to think about it. I look at what God has created here on earth and know heaven is so much better than what we can see. God knows everything—what has happened, what will happen. I trust that He knew what was best for Riley. God keeps His word and makes everything work together so that we may be better people. He takes care of us. He had a purpose for Riley. One day his short life will make sense to me. Was his purpose for me to help others go through this grieving process? Was it for our faith during this to be shown to others? Will this bring others to Christ? In time, I think God will reveal His perfect plan.

Mom and Dad are back from the reunion. I missed them so much. I missed not being able to go to their house to escape and get away from the constant stream of company that comes to my house. When I am at their house, I do not have to pretend that I am okay. I can just be myself.

Today, I decided to go through Riley's clothes. I just knew someone was going to stop by and find me a crying mess. But I needed that time to cry by myself. It was a sad, but special, time for me. It was also a growing time for me. It's in times like these that I really feel God comforting me. I feel His peace.

September 17, 1990

I have had such a hectic week. I have tried slowing down, and I think that is why today was good. I cleaned the house and took time to really enjoy Katie and Taylor.

Today felt like fall and I love it! Fall makes me happy. This summer has been like a roller coaster for me with a lot of ups and downs. I am glad for a change of season. I took time out to thank God for the seasons. Seasons of weather, but also seasons of life. Seasons to grow and seasons to reflect. This past season has been a time to grieve and trust. I am ready for a new season.

Taylor starts school soon, and I am ready to start fall cleaning and prepping my yard for the spring. I love a change in season!

Brian and I are having a sketch done of Riley. I cannot wait to see the finished product.

At a friend's house, I saw a beautiful picture of Jesus in a book. I wondered if this is what Riley sees every day. We don't know what Jesus really looks like, but when I looked at that picture, I was comforted. It made me happy knowing my baby is with Him.

We passed an ambulance, and Brian and I both thought of Riley.

One of my friends just found out she is pregnant. I think she was a little worried to tell me. I congratulated her, even though it was so difficult for me. I get sad thinking of not having another baby. I always wanted four kids. That was before I had twins.

At McDonald's, I met a lady I never want to see again. She told me about a friend of hers that just had twins. She told me that her friend did everything right in her pregnancy, and she stayed in bed so the babies would be healthy. I let her know I was on bed rest for six weeks and that I had healthy babies too. But I told her I lost one of my twins. She did not take the hint to be quiet. She went on to tell me how adorable her friends' babies are and told me how cute they are when they sleep in the same bed. I almost lost it! This lady had no clue how insensitive she was being and how much she was hurting me. I hope I never make anyone feel the way she made me feel.

We have been to several Reynolds football games. Brian loves taking Taylor. I know Katie loves going to these too. Everyone wants to hold her. I love doing things as a family. We try to live life to the fullest—no matter the circumstances. We will never forget Riley. We still think of Riley, but instead of always being sad, I think of how blessed we are, and I cherish the time we have together.

Today, Katie wore her fuzzy bunny slippers. Riley had a matching pair. It has been three months since he died. At times, it seems like it just happened. At other times, it feels like it was so long ago.

I wrote to a friend today, and I wanted to include a picture of the kids. It didn't feel right to include one without Riley. I guess we will never have a complete family picture until we get to heaven.

Someone told me to think of Riley like I would a friend or relative on an extended vacation. That person is happy and having fun. You miss them, but you are content knowing they are enjoying themselves. Sometimes, I think of Riley that way. He is safe, happy, and being very well taken care of. I love you, Riley!

I sometimes feel like I have to be upbeat when I do not feel like being upbeat. I know people would get tired of being around me if I were always depressed. Good friends understand, but I am sure seeing me depressed gets old. I want to be happy and make my life count. A lot easier said than done, but I am doing my best. It seems as time goes by, I talk less about the twins. When I see twins, I have a hard time. When I see a double stroller, I breathe a sigh of relief when I see two children instead of twins. I hope these things will get easier. I don't enjoy having those feelings. It hurts. I was the mom who was so proud of her twins. Their birth was such an amazing miracle. If I went to heaven today, I would want to see Riley first. God would understand; He has a Son too. I wish I could see Riley's smile.

Good night, Riley. I love you.

Sometime in September 1990

At 3:00 p.m., I decided to highlight my hair and perm the back. This was a very bad idea. A perm and highlights are not supposed to be done on the same day. I know this. But I called Mom to borrow her big hair dryer, came home, and dyed and permed my hair. I am now under the hair dryer with a deep conditioning hair treatment because my hair is fried! Maybe this will keep me from going completely bald. This sure beats sitting around being depressed.

Tonight at dinner, Brian told me he has been thinking. I am not sure if this is good or bad, but I like that he opened up a little to me. He told me he thought back to when Dr. Rice told us that Riley had died. Just remembering that tears both of us up. We miss him so much. I cannot believe that at age twenty-five, I have lost a child.

I heard Dave Dravecky on a show today. What a testimony he has! I am sure God is pleased with his amazing outlook on life. He has been through so much but remains faithful to God. I hope one day, I can have that outlook too. I don't always say the right thing; I still have so much to learn. It is still hard for me to pray.

It's time to do a fall family photo. It is going to be so hard. A year ago, we never would have dreamed we would be going through this. I would have never wanted to see my future. I now know why God does not show us. If I knew ahead of time that I would lose one of my babies, I would not have wanted to live. I would have never gotten pregnant, and I never would have experienced the joy of Katie or Taylor. That would have been awful. I do not want to know what the future holds. I want to live for today!

September 30, 1990

So much has been going on. I have been so busy being a mom. Listening to Bill Gaither sing "Because He Lives" makes me cry every time. It gives me hope and reminds me that with Christ, I can face what may come my way. I am so glad that when I have a bad day, God gives me a tomorrow. A fresh new day. Joy comes in the morning.

We had a crazy weekend. We went to Burlington, North Carolina, for Brian's cousin's wedding. He married a girl who is a twin. At the reception, they displayed pictures of the two girls as babies. It was so hard to see those. I was sad to think Katie will not have her twin at her wedding. I not only grieve the loss of a son, but the loss of a twin. I will always get a reminder when Katie does something for the first time or when she celebrates a birthday. I will always wonder what Riley would be doing. The void Riley left is deep.

Taylor caught the garter at the wedding. He was the only single male! I think it would be cute for him to give that to Katie when she gets married. It could be her "something blue."

October 8, 1990

I cannot believe it is almost Halloween. Time flies by so fast.

Dad still gets weepy if we mention Riley. He acts tough, but deep down, he is a softie.

Brian told me he is still thinking of Riley. He said he worries about Katie and Taylor. If something were to happen to either of them, he would not be able to handle it. I feel the same way. It was such a terrible feeling when Dr. Rice told us there was nothing they could do for Riley. We could not bear that again.

I remember being with Riley in the hospital. I had to hold him one last time. He looked so perfect—just like he did when he was alive. Brian said a prayer. Taylor just stared. We told Taylor we would see Riley again one day. I wonder what he was think-ing and what he understood. We all gave Riley a kiss before we left. It was a precious moment.

I think I miss Riley's smile the most. I still hurt a lot at times, but those times are getting further apart. When Riley died, I did not want to live. I didn't want to go to sleep because I knew I would relive everything when I woke up. It took all I had to go from day to day. I am happy to say I now have more happy days than sad days. When I do have a Riley day, it takes me by surprise.

10

I love going to Riley's Rock. He is buried under a big tree. It is a place for me to reflect.

What I have learned so far is that so many people are hurting, babies and children with cancer or other serious problems. I would hate to see one of my children suffer every day. I know God comforts them like He has my family. When faced with such a tragedy, God shows up with amazing miracles.

Someone once said to me, "God must have known that the two of you could handle the loss of a child better than someone else." This is not how God works. God allowed this tragedy to happen for His good. God sees the big picture of our lives. We may not see His purpose, but it is there. He gives us what we need when we need it. He gives us peace, comfort, love, and hope. Riley's death was for a purpose. Brian and I may be able to help someone else who has lost a child.

Good night, Riley!

October 11, 1990

It is a rainy and dark day. The wind is blowing like crazy, and leaves are all over the place. I am curled up on the couch with a quilt eating popcorn and drinking sweet tea. The kids are napping. It is so great to have days like this. It gives me an excuse to stay inside and be lazy.

Riley has been on my mind so much lately. I am sure he has grown so much. I want to see what he looks like. Brian and I still cannot believe he is not coming back.

Sometimes I wonder if Brian and I are okay. I always want both he and the kids to know how much they mean to me. I know I can be moody sometimes. And sometimes, I yell when I am upset. I don't want to be that way. I don't know if the moodiness is really sadness. I am not sure. Sometimes, I don't want to talk. I just want to be left alone.

Brian is wonderful for me. I love his smile. He has the greatest smile. He is sensitive and attentive to my needs. He never complains when I need his help. He always wants to be with me. He understands me and doesn't take things personally when I am not always nice or when I am upset. Brian is good at everything! He's never met a stranger, and everyone likes him. I am so proud to be his wife. I asked him if he would get remarried if something were to happen to me. He said no but that he would want to be there for Katie and Taylor. They would be his top priority. I hate to think of Brian with someone else, but I would want him to be happy. I love Brian more than anyone in this world. He always makes me feel safe. He is smart and handsome and has such a love for God. He is my best friend. I always want to be with him, and when we are apart, I miss him so much. I look forward to growing old with him. I am so fortunate to have such a wonderful husband.

Taylor just walked in and got under the quilt with me. He is so cuddly—and so sweet! Sometimes he bugs Katie, but he takes care of her too. Katie adores Taylor too. As long as Taylor is in the room, she is fine. Katie is so funny! She is so tiny, but she makes me laugh so much. She stands up in her crib and says "Dada" over and over. She has her bottom two teeth. She still wants me to hold her all of the time. I am so fortunate to be able to stay home with her; it is the most rewarding job in the world. I am not sure how long I can stay home with the kids, but I love every minute I get to be with them.

My biggest fear is something happening to either of my children. I will never get over losing one child. I worry most when I go to bed. Someone told me that as soon as I start to worry, I should pray. That works. I feel better knowing God never sleeps, and He is watching over my kids.

I have not been walking the Christian walk lately. I know I should. I am trying, though. I surround myself with people who lift me up and help me grow. I want to be like God and for God to be proud of me. Sometimes, I just get into a daze, and I realize God is the only reason I am functioning. I feel like part of me is missing. Life can be so overwhelming at times.

Katie is now up from her nap, and Brian will be home soon. He will see that we did not get much done today. He doesn't care.

Good night, Riley! I love you.

November 11, 1990

I cannot believe how long it has been since I have written in my journal.

Mom, Dad, Brian, Taylor, and I went to Atlanta last weekend. We had so much fun visiting Tim. Mary watched Katie for us. We took Taylor to the Atlanta Zoo, and he loved all of the animals. We ate at the Varsity. Mom and Dad took Taylor for the rest of the day so Brian and I could have some much needed alone time. The next day, we went to the Ramblin' Wreck Parade at Georgia Tech. We had a very busy weekend but had so much fun!

Brian and I started going to Trinity Presbyterian Church, and I love it! It is the first time in years that I have been excited to go to church. I have been a Christian since I was seven, so I did not have that "come to Jesus" moment that so many people talk about. In high school, I remember thinking I did not have an exciting testimony. But my decision was special to me, and it was real. I don't feel like I have grown lately. Nor have I wanted to. But I know that God never left me and was always waiting for me to come back to Him.

I have always gone to church because if you are a Christian, you go to church. You go where your parents take you. I rarely got anything out of church. I know it was my attitude—not the church or the people in the church. You believe what your parents say. But you have to believe for yourself.

I have always prayed and thought I was a good Christian, but I stopped growing a long time ago. My growing was never consistent. I never had a deep desire to read my Bible. Some days, I made God a priority, and other days, I did not acknowledge Him. When I did something wrong, the Holy Spirit was always there to let me know.

I once heard a speaker say she keeps a chair in her bedroom, and she calls it her Jesus chair. It reminds her that Jesus is sitting patiently, waiting to talk with her. Jesus has been waiting to spend time with me for so long. I have been too busy for Him.

It took the death of Riley for me to come back to the Jesus I trusted when I was seven. I tested God. I asked Him to reveal himself to me. He did in so many ways. The strength, comfort, peace, and hope that I have experienced can only come from God. I am so glad He never left me or has never forsaken me. He is the calm in my storm—the peace that passes all understanding. He just wants a relationship with us. I have to give God credit for carrying me through the loss of Riley. I could not do that on my own. God is the only way Brian and I are making it through this. We would not be able to go on if it were not for Him.

Mom has started a Bible study group. It is a small group of women, and it will be a nice, intimate group. I know I need the support of other Christian women.

I have been feeling so insecure with Brian lately. I have been so moody lately. I am up one minute and down the next. Poor Brian! I have also been very weepy. I am sure it is because I feel so guilty about my attitude. I haven't been able to talk about Riley without crying.

Katie has been fussy lately too. I hope it's just the diaper rash. Mom and I hosted a Halloween party for Taylor and his friends. Everyone dressed up, and it was so fun! Taylor had a clown nose and wig and was so funny. Katie was a lion with whiskers on her face. She was too adorable to scare anyone!

I really want to visit Riley's grave, but it is so hard with two little ones. The other night, Taylor said we needed to bring Riley back. I pray he will understand one day. I love you, Riley. I know your presence in heaven has made it even more of a beautiful place. I know you are growing into a beautiful little Brian. Good night, Riley!

Brian just got home, and the kids are in bed. Going to go spend time with him.

Good night, Riley!

December 16, 1990

At the moment, I feel pretty good. The last few days, I scared myself. I have never been this depressed. I started thinking about how the family would fare without me. They'd be okay, right? They don't need me. Those thoughts were awful. It was so hard to block them out. I think with the holidays coming, it's making my depression worse.

Christmas has always been my favorite holiday, but I am dreading it this year. This would have been the twins' first Christmas, and their birthday is coming up next month. I really want to enjoy the holidays, but I cannot shake this sadness. I need to be happy for Katie and Taylor.

December 17, 1990

Today was one of the most special days. We took the kids to Claxton Farm, which was set up like a live nativity. We walked in the barn to see Mary, Joseph, and baby Jesus. Shepherds were in the fields with sheep. They also had a camel and a donkey. While I was holding Katie, she reached out and grabbed the camel's tongue! She wasn't afraid of him at all! She was only interested in the animals. Taylor just wanted to see baby Jesus.

Tonight made me focus on the real meaning of Christmas. It was good for all of us. I love Santa, but I want the kids to understand the true meaning of Christmas.

December 18, 1990

I am relaxing in the tub and enjoying the quiet and calm.

Mary stopped by today and brought Katie a cute Christmas outfit. We will go to the Parks' house tomorrow, and Katie will wear her outfit there. I have noticed Katie being aggressive with other babies. I think it's because of Riley.

The song "Leaving on a Jet Plane" just came on the radio. I feel like jumping on that plane and taking a trip to heaven to visit Riley. I wish it were that easy! Sometimes, I look to the sky hoping God will give me a peek at what Riley looks like these days. I will keep looking.

The situation in Iraq is still in waiting. I hurt for those families that have family in Saudi Arabia. I pray they come home soon.

I am still taking jazz classes. Our teacher says she wants our class to be in the recital at the end of the season. Diane and I started cracking up! We knew we would sell so many tickets to our friends and family who would pay to see the two of us dancing on stage. How funny we would look! Hee-hee! Even though we said we would not do it, our teacher made us order the costumes—just in case we changed our minds. We haven't yet! We could not imagine us in a recital—two moms. And Diane is newly pregnant!

I am happy that Diane is pregnant. I think it is so exciting! I have to say, it kind of makes me want to have another baby. It would be really complicated; I know this is not going to happen.

Katie and Taylor are really close. I hope they will always be close and need each other.

Taylor helped me make cookies. He said, "Mommy, when I'm big like you, I will chop nuts too."

Taylor spent the night with Mom and Dad. They just got a king-size bed. Taylor asked where they got it. Mom said in Hickory. Taylor says he wants a tiny bed—and he wants it from Dickory Dock too. He is so funny and says the cutest things!

While driving Katie and Taylor the other day, I got a sick feeling in my stomach. What would I do if they were not here? They are the world to me!

Brian and I love our new church. I really feel the love of God in that church. Everyone is so nice.

At Taylor's Christmas program, a two-year-old sang "Rudolph the Red Nosed Reindeer." It was so cute but made me think of Riley. I miss Riley so much. He is always on my mind. I wish he were here for Katie. Before he died, I always thought how great it would be for the twins to go to school together. They would have had each other for support. If Riley were crying, I would lay Katie next to him in the crib, and he would stop crying. They needed each other.

Mom came over Monday through Friday morning to help with feeding and bathing the twins, then with their naps. Don't want to get them off schedule! She loved it! We always had so much fun picking out their matching outfits! This also allowed me to have "Taylor Time."

Riley, I love you and miss you. I know it must be special celebrating Jesus's birthday with Him in heaven. You are so lucky! I look forward to seeing you again. The holidays will not be the same without you. I love you, little guy!

11

December 23, 1990

The doorbell rang, and we sent Taylor to answer it. Santa Claus was at our door! Taylor looked at Santa and then looked back at us. It was priceless! I had been waiting all day for our special guest to arrive, and I think I was more excited than anyone else.

Taylor got some milk and a few of our cookies for Santa. Taylor was able to tell Santa what he wanted for Christmas. He just could not believe Santa was at his house—two days before Christmas!

Katie wanted nothing to do with Santa. She screamed every time he came close. I think it hurt his heart a little. Santa goes to our church, and everyone loves him. He was not used to kids not liking him. Katie will grow to love Santa, I just know it!

It was so nice. Mrs. Claus told us she used a glue gun to adhere Santa's eyebrows. Mom and I could not even begin to imagine the pain when he takes those off! I will definitely never forget this special visit.

December 28, 1990

I am so glad Christmas is over. I never thought I would be saying that. It was so hard. I think the anticipation for a holiday is harder than the actual day. I always dread the day, but when it gets here, it is somehow okay. I know how important Christmas is, and I know that as time goes on, it will get easier for me. This time last year, I was at Mom and Dad's on bed rest. It was such an exciting time.

The twins' birthday is in just a few weeks. I wish Riley were here. I would have loved to see Katie and Riley together on their first Christmas. Everything Katie does, I always picture Riley doing the same.

Taylor was so cute at Christmas. He was so excited about all of the presents he got. He kept thanking everyone and giving out hugs. He got a train, a basketball goal, an ice cream set, a bear, a tape recorder with a microphone, clothes, books, and the Cooties game. The train was the biggest hit! He is such a great age, and I enjoyed making Christmas cookies and ornaments with him.

Katie got spoiled. She got her first Cabbage Patch Kid (the first of many to come), a Minnie Mouse doll, stuffed animals, a rocking horse, books, and clothes. She has been sick with an ear infection, so she wasn't feeling her best but was excited about all that Santa brought. It cracks me up how she jabbers to her dolls. I pray I have the relationship with her that my mom and I have.

Good night, Riley!

December 31, 1990

Tomorrow starts 1991. As I reflect over this last year, I cannot believe what we have been through. It makes me sad to think I had a baby in 1990 who is no longer with us. I would love to start this New

Year with all three of my kids. I will never forget the happiness Riley brought to my life.

I know Katie's birthday will be hard, probably the hardest day so far. I wish Katie had her twin to celebrate their day together.

I love Katie so much! She is so tiny, yet so energetic.

My prayer for 1991 is that I stop worrying so much. I am just so afraid that I will lose Brian or one of the kids. I have learned so much this past year. I hope I will continue to grow closer to God. I pray that I am a good wife and a good role model for my kids.

I am almost to the last page in this journal. I feel like part of Riley will be gone when I finish this journal. It has helped so much. I have so many feelings written in this book. It has helped me deal with my loss. Riley will always be in my heart and in my thoughts.

To my Riley, a lot has happened. I love you, little guy, more than I could have ever imagined. You are the son I will always dream about. Dreams of what you would have been, what you would look like, what fun we would have had together, what sports you would have played, what kind of hair you would have had.

Maybe you are seeing things in heaven that I will someday see. You will never be forgotten. Our family will always talk about you. We will share our loss. I hope you know how much we love and miss you. No one will ever take your place. It gives me comfort to know that even in heaven, no one will replace me as your mommy.

I love you more than yesterday, and my love for you will never stop growing. It is hard to think I could love you more than the day you were born, but I do. I cannot wait to see you at the gates of heaven waiting for me.

Good night, Riley!

January 2, 1991

When I finished writing in my first journal, I had such sadness. When I closed it, I felt like I was leaving part of Riley behind. This past year was about tears, hurt, pain, loss, and sadness. I look back at those first months after our Riley died and remember how hard it was.

My journal was my way of writing to Riley and expressing how I was feeling. So many pages were smeared from my tears.

I was so scared I would forget what Riley looked like. I did not want to forget how perfectly he fit into my arms. I did not want to forget the wonderful months we had with him. I did not want to forget anything about him. I wanted to make sure I wrote it all down so I could tell Katie about her twin.

The day before Riley died, our family room was full of laughter. The grandparents stopped by. Close friends came by. One of my clients wanted to see the twins before she moved across the world. She snapped a picture of Taylor with the twins—not knowing how precious that last photo would be. No one knew it was Riley's last day on earth. God knew it would be Riley's last day. God knew it would be a special day. Everyone was able to spend time holding each of the kids.

Taylor will never know how much he helped me during this time. He seemed to always know when

I needed a hug or cuddle time. On one of my "Riley Days," I stepped into the bathroom so Taylor would not see me crying. After a few minutes, Taylor pushed a card made from construction paper under the door.

I opened the door and gave him the biggest hug. And, I cried some more. Taylor said he didn't want me to be sad. When I said I cried because I missed Riley, he simply said, "I know, Mommy." I stopped crying and told Taylor it was because of his card. He felt so much better knowing he made me feel better. He has such a gentle heart.

This past year has been hard on Brian too. He had to be strong for us but had to keep up with his daily duties. Life seems to keep on going—no matter what the circumstances. While I had time to sit and mourn, Brian had to continue working to pay our bills. I am sure he didn't want to go in every day. I know those first few days back to work were tough on him. He could not escape his pain while at work.

God knew what He was doing. He knew that when I was in seventh grade, I would meet the man who would hold me when I cried myself to sleep at night. He knew I needed Brian. He was so tender, compassionate, understanding, and patient with me.

Brian waited so patiently for intimacy to return to our relationship. I realize it is important to meet your husband's physical needs, but I was not ready for that for a long time after Riley died. He never pressured me. I knew that I had to make myself be intimate with him. It was a first step to something we enjoyed before Riley died. We needed each other. It was so important to put the other's needs before our own—to restore what had become lost.

January 6, 1991

I miss you, Riley. I wish I had you to hold. I wish you were here for your first birthday. I love you!

January 19, 1991

Katie is one year old today! She is so cute! She has long eyelashes, and everyone melts when they look at her. But she barely has any hair! Taylor has thick blonde curls, and Katie has fuzz! She is constantly jabbering and singing. I have no clue what she is saying, but she is so cute!

We had a birthday party at Mom and Dad's. I knew it was going to be a bittersweet day, but this was her day. I wanted to be thankful for the joy she brings me. I think all of the family had to hold back tears as we sang "Happy Birthday." It was so obvious that Riley was missing, but we all tried to be strong.

I told Taylor that Riley was having a birthday party in heaven. We talked about how much fun that would be. We lit a candle for Riley and let Taylor blow it out. It will be something we do every year.

We had a cake for Katie. At first, she was not sure what to do, but once she tasted icing, we could not stop her! Her face was sweeter than ever.

Katie's birthday outfit was all pink! She had on leggings with a long pink and white polka dot sweatshirt with a ruffle at the bottom. Her hat was pink and white polka dots. She is such a princess!

At age one, Katie's day includes a good morning kiss, a diaper change (how can someone so cute and small be so stinky!), breakfast, running around in the walker looking for Taylor or play in the playroom (she loves to pull out all of her toys), bathing and dressing for the day, brushing her two teeth, juice and snack, nap if we are at home, going to aerobics, running errands, visiting Grandma or play with Maggie, lunch, nap time, cuddle time with Mommy, snack, playing with Taylor, watching a Barney tape, helping Mommy in the kitchen or play babies, dinner, and waiting for Daddy. Daddy time is so special. She gets so excited when Brian comes home from work. He is such a great dad and spends time with the kids before he does anything else.

We are a tag team once Brian gets home. After he says hello to the kids, he helps me with whatever I need. If I do the dishes, he helps Katie get ready for bed. He reads Taylor his devotion before he tucks him in. The sooner we get the kids to bed, the sooner we are able to have our time together.

Riley, I want to say Happy Birthday! I think about you all of the time. Every time your sister does something new, I think of you. I miss you and cannot wait to see you one day. I bet you have so much hair. I am sure you are looking more and more like your daddy. One day, our family will be together again. For now, I need to be here to take care of Katie and Taylor, but you will always be a part of us. I will never feel complete until I see you again. What a happy day that will be! During this past year, I have learned so much about the importance of life and family because of you. It is so precious! As I write, I cannot stop crying. I wish I could just have one glimpse of you. I wonder if when you are older, God will let you see us and our happy moments. Happy first birthday!

I love you!

12

February 1, 1991

I started back to work with a hair salon in my house so I could work from home with the kids. This was my first time working since Riley died.

When one of my first clients came and sat in my chair, she asked how Brian and I were doing. She didn't know I was thinking of leaving him. I had been thinking about it for a while. Mostly because I felt like Brian needed someone else. He needed someone whole—not someone broken. And he hadn't really seemed to be very sad about Riley. He actually stopped asking me about my grief.

I am so thankful Alice came in that day to get a haircut. She said, "It breaks my heart to see Brian on his lunch break."

Since I knew Brian packed his lunch every day, I asked where she saw him. "He has lunch in his truck at Riley's grave."

Alice works at the church where Riley is buried. We call it Riley's Rock—and she could see Brian through her office window. I almost lost it! Brian was hurting, and he was grieving the only way he knew how. He was being so strong when he came home from work. I just thought he was not sad, but he didn't want to make me sad by asking about Riley.

When Brian got home from work that evening, I had a new love for him. God put Alice in my chair at the time I was thinking of leaving my husband. I was so certain he didn't care about Riley. Alice had no clue how important her haircut was to me that day.

We never know how God will use us in other people's lives. God knew exactly what I needed to hear that day when Alice sat in my chair. Satan never had a chance!

I always encourage couples to get counseling when they lose a child. It is so much better than hitting rock bottom like I did. Our grief was slowly destroying our marriage.

Looking back, this hurts to write. I cannot imagine my life without Brian. I want to grow old with him. I want to be grandparents with him. I want to be with him until the day God is ready to take me home.

February 12, 1991

I am so thankful for both my parents and Brian's parents. I love having them in our kids' lives. They were such a huge help last year and helped us in so many ways.

Dad is such an incredible man. He tries so hard to be strong, and I know he still hurts when I hurt. He stayed at the hospital when Taylor was in critical condition. He was always at the hospital with Riley. I know he misses him so much. I'm so thankful that he's there whenever he can be. Taylor loves being with him, especially when Dad helped remodel the house. Taylor was there right by his side, with his own little tools and tool belt. He watches everything Dad does and says, "Poppy can do it!"

I'm so thankful that he and Mom let us crash at their house before we had the twins. I'm so thankful for the beautiful wicker bassinet he repaired for Katie and Riley. He's the most talented man I have ever known. My dad can do anything.

Dad was known as the Wicker Man in Asheville. Everyone wanted my dad to repair old wicker furniture that had been their parents', grandparents', or even great-grandparents'.

One of the highlights of dad's life was when he was asked to repair wicker for Ruth and Billy Graham. When he delivered the wicker, Ruth invited him and mom to tea. They shared stories about their family and ministry.

My mom has been through so much with me. Words cannot even begin to say how much I love and appreciate all she's done to help me have three healthy babies. She always gave so much of herself and truly is an example of a Proverbs 31 woman. She's beautiful inside and out. She taught me how to make memories. I love how we can quickly go from crying to laughing. I love when we are supposed to be running errands and we end up getting coffee and looking at houses.

She showed me how to be a mom. I was so scared, but she knew I could do it. She put her life on hold to help me with mine. One of my favorite memories is her coming over for bath time with the kids. We had babies everywhere; we loved it! She is constantly showing me how to make a house a home.

I pray that I can be half the woman she is. I pray that one day I make memories with my grandchildren like she has with Katie and Taylor. She's always believed in me. She knows me and understands when I have Riley Days. She always knows what to say and what to do.

Hal is such a patient man; I'm so blessed to have him as my father-in-law. Taylor loves his "Paw-Paw" time. He makes washing the car and working in the yard fun. He is always taking the time to explain things to Taylor. His life is so busy at home, so when he gives him undivided attention, he feels so special. He's always encouraging him, and for that, I am forever grateful. When our life was so hectic and we were trying to cope, he made sure Taylor did not feel left out.

Mary is a wonderful mother-in-law. She jumps in whenever we needed her. She always watched Taylor at a moment's notice. It was so nice not to have to get a babysitter. I am so appreciative of her help when I was on bed rest. It gave Mom a break from a toddler and Taylor a break from Mom. I appreciate all of her help with the twins. She made so many trips to and from the hospital. Riley and Taylor were both so blessed to have such a crowd watching over them in the neonatal nursery. I will always cherish the quilts she made for Riley and Katie. I love her most for having a son who I adore and for whom I give thanks every single day.

13

March 28, 1993

Oh my goodness! It's been such a long time since I have written in my journal. I have been so busy! But I bought this beautiful journal, and it has inspired me. I have missed my writing time. I cannot believe I have not written in over a year and a half! So much has been going on.

Taylor loved his Pre-K class so much. When it was time to move to kindergarten, we were not sure he was ready. He was one of the youngest in his class. The teacher told us that he is the sweetest, most adorable, and most caring child she has ever had in her class. She said Taylor is so secure because of the love Brian and I share. He is so happy and doesn't have a care in the world. His nickname is Smiley. I cannot believe he will be in kindergarten soon. Brian and I are so lucky to have such a sweet little boy. And we are lucky he loves his little sister so much too!

Taylor has a hard time letting us down. It is so hard to discipline him when he does something wrong. He gets so upset when he knows he has upset us.

Right now, Taylor is so creative! He loves building remarkable things from Legos. He draws all the time and loves using tape and glue.

Taylor also likes to sneak into our bed at night. While it makes me feel so secure to have him next to me, I know it is not best. I also feel like a grump when I do not get a full night's rest. We have learned to toughen up and put him back in his bed when he comes to ours.

These days, Taylor is spending a lot of time with his Paw-Paw. They play together at least once a week. When he retired from the bank, Paw-Paw became a bus driver, and Taylor gets to ride along if it is going to be a short ride. Taylor also loves to help him in the yard and take things to the dump. Paw-Paw is teaching Taylor to ride a bike and use a computer. And together, they pulled down Brian's old race tracks and enjoy zooming cars around! Taylor loves this special time.

April 30, 1993

After Riley's death, I couldn't continue to work as a hairstylist. I tried, but it wasn't the same. I wanted to be with my children as much as I could.

I started painting kid-friendly animals and stick figures on T-shirts and sweatshirts to make a little extra money. Everyone loves the designs! I've been painting anytime I have a free minute. Now, I have over 125 shirts ordered! There's shirts laid out to dry on every surface in the house!

I can't keep doing everything by hand. I had to find a way to fill shirt orders faster. Mom and I put our heads together and came up with a plan. I would design the shirts, and we would have them screen printed. The turnover would be so much faster. Plus, I could spend more time with Taylor and Katie.

Mom is such an incredible artist and can make anything! We decided to go into business together and "Animal Crackers" was born. Because of copyright issues, Animal Crackers had to be changed. We took inspiration from the way Taylor said "animal." Our new business was renamed "Aminal Factory." We rented an old house and redid it to make it into a children's boutique. Taylor and Katie had both a bunk room and a playroom. It was perfect!

Katie was the store model. When anyone would see her outfits, they just had to have them! Customers would even ask Katie which outfit was her favorite. She would show them the dresses and T-shirts that she liked. She was quite the salesman—and she was only two feet tall!

When I see Katie I can't help but wonder what she and Riley would look like in matching Aminal Factory outfits. My mind wanders for a little while, and then Katie hollers for me. She helps me snap back to the present.

Our business started taking off. We would both design the graphics and pick out the fabrics, and Mom made the patterns to be sewn. Soon, we started designing our own fabrics. We also needed more hands. We found others moms who could sew who wanted to work from home. We got sales reps from all over the US!

Mom and I went to the Atlanta Market to showcase Aminal Factory—an experience I will never forget. A friend suggested we dress the part. Mom and I wore huge hair bows, oversized T-shirts with leggings, and Converse high tops. We could not stop laughing at ourselves!

While at Market, I was both excited and nervous. When our first customer came by, I ducked behind the table and left Mom on her own. But I was stuck with the next customer; there was nowhere to hide! While we did not get many orders at the show, we did win Best of Show and received red roses and a ribbon.

Three years later, Aminal Factory got a call asking us to design bedding for a large company. After many meetings, we decided to close our store and design exclusively for this company. After a few months of royalty checks, the company filed bankruptcy, and the millions the company promised never came. Aminal Factory was finished.

We took our closing pretty hard. We had worked so hard for so long. We were crushed. But you can't look back. God closed that door for a reason.

Aminal Factory was good for me because it kept my mind off Riley. I was excited about our new adventure. I was moving forward even though I missed Riley so much.

May 28, 1993

The kids had so much fun in the baby pool today, especially when they added Taylor's "choo-choo" slide. I love watching them play together; they are so close.

The last time I wrote in my journal, I spent so much time writing what Taylor is doing. I thought I would use today to share what Katie is doing now.

Katie has the Adams' personality and is always joking around. But she is also a cuddle bug who loves to give hugs and kisses. The first thing she does when she wakes up from a nap is run to me for hugs and kisses. Plus, she always wakes up in a good mood. She sleeps hard and plays hard.

Katie always asks me to tell her stories about Riley and what he did when he was alive. I tell her how much Riley loved her and how being next to her made him smile. She always made his eyes light up. She laughs when I tell her Riley liked to suck her fingers or hold onto her ear. One day, I will tell her more stories.

I love my Katie Bug!

June 1, 1993

Today, Katie let me know she would like to see Riley in heaven. Not knowing what exactly to say to a three-and-a-half-year-old, I explained that we cannot see him until Jesus comes to get us. She needed to know how we will go to heaven.

"We will all hold hands and go to heaven together with Jesus," I told her.

"Okay, Mommy," she replied.

I thought the conversation was over.

Later that day, she told Mom, "Gramma, when we go to heaven, Jesus will hold Mommy and Daddy's hand, and I will hold their hands, and so will Taylor, Gramma, Poppy, Granny, Paw-Paw, and Aunt Jean. But Molly can't go!" Molly is Jean's dog. Katie explained that since Molly has no hands, she cannot go with us. Katie is always saying the funniest things!

Katie is very petite and has blue eyes with double eyelashes. She can tear up in seconds, and it crushes my heart—and Brian is worse! Katie is also very social and enjoys chatting with everyone. She thinks everyone is coming to see her.

I gave Katie a haircut. It is short in the back and longer in the front and frames her face. People are constantly asking who cut her hair and what the style is called. I call it "The Katie."

Her favorite color is pink, and her hero is Barney, the big purple dinosaur. She loves to play with makeup and dress up. We have so much fun together!

Katie is a little strong-willed, and she is very persistent. I always prayed my kids would be confident, and I am so thankful they are!

Katie and Taylor are both crazy about Brian. Since he works late, he usually comes home in time to do their nightly devotions with them. This is their special time with their daddy.

Sometimes I think about having another baby. It makes me so anxious. I always thought I would have a big family, but I know God knows best. I pray this desire goes away and that I find peace.

September 12, 1993

What a weekend! Brian and I had our five-year class reunion, and it was so much fun! We danced the night away!

The deejay asked for a couple to go to the dance floor. Everyone "volunteered" us. He explained we would play a game. When the music started, Brian and I had to dance. When it stopped, we had to grab someone from the crowd to dance with while the music played. When it stopped again, we had to grab someone else—until the whole crowd was dancing. This made me a little uncomfortable. Who would I grab? Who would Brian grab?

I grabbed a man from the crowd I did not think would be dancing otherwise. Brian grabbed two sisters—girls who would always joke with me in high school about "stealing my man." I laughed so hard! Brian was moving like I had never seen him move! Dancing is so not his thing! I have no clue what I looked like because I was laughing so hard! Laughter is so good for the soul.

Brian was so sweet to me this evening. He kept staring at me and telling me how beautiful I looked. He is always so attentive! He looked so handsome in his suit. We just smiled when people said we didn't look any older than we did in high school. That was so nice to hear!

God, thank you for bringing Brian and I together in seventh grade—fourteen years ago! I love him so much! Please help us keep our eyes on you and keep you in the center of our marriage.

October 23, 1993

It's almost midnight, and I had a few thoughts on my mind that I wanted to write down.

A few days ago, Brian built Taylor a tree house. The kids played in it for two hours. Why didn't we build this sooner! They talked and pretended, and it was so sweet! Taylor is so patient with his little sister, and she loves him and looks up to him. Sometimes, I wonder if Taylor feels left out because he was not a twin. I would never want him to feel that way! He is such a huge part of Katie's life.

Taylor recently told me he shared God with Katie. He told her how to let Jesus into her heart.

He is planting the seed in his little sister, and that is incredible to watch!

Mom is great about helping with the kids. Katie has started taking dance—in her black leotard and pink ballet slippers. She never lets me forget when she has dance.

I have realized how important relationships are, and I try so hard not to take them for granted. People can be so fragile. You never know what others are going through or have gone through in their lives. A lot of times, we compare ourselves to others and want what they have. We never know what they may have that they keep hidden.

When we keep our friends in a tight circle, we miss out on so much. We miss blessings of other friends, but we may also miss an opportunity to help someone in need. Sometimes we don't build a relationship because we are too busy and cannot find time. Take time to look around and pay attention when God lays someone on your heart. I want less of me and more of God.

Lord, help me be content with what I have. Always remind me of the incredible family you have given me. It is priceless. Let me show my love by example to Katie and Taylor. Thank you, God!

October 31, 1993

Halloween is now over. The kids loved getting dressed up and getting candy. Mom made the kids' costumes. Taylor was a candy bar, and Katie was Tinker Bell. Taylor glued pieces of candy to his hat and it was a huge hit! I'm sure all the kids were tempted to eat his hat. Katie was so cute a lady asked if she could video tape her. My kids are just so sweet and do not have a mean bone in their little bodies.

A few days ago, the house was really quiet. When I looked for the kids, I couldn't find them. When I finally found Taylor, he looked worried. Then I saw Katie. Taylor decided to cut Katie's hair with my clippers! It is not pretty at all! Katie has bald spots all over her head! Why does this happen around the holidays? I don't think Taylor will do that again. What a family Christmas card photo this will be!

Brian and I have decided we will not have any more children. I know it is the right thing to do.

Good night, Riley! I will never ever forget you!

14

November 29, 1993

It's Thanksgiving! What a full day we have. We have to get the kids up and ready, watch the Rose Bowl Parade, and get food ready for Brian's family Thanksgiving at 1:00 p.m. and my family's Thanksgiving at 7:00 p.m. Then I will lie on my back feeling miserable thinking about all of the food I just consumed. We do this every year, and this year should not be any different!

Once we got to Mom's, Brian got a pile of cookies and poured a glass of sweet tea. Then he settled in to watch all of the football of the day. The men always watch football, while the women are in the kitchen cooking away. The men seem to forget anything else going on around them. They may comment on the aroma of food cooking or sample a piece of turkey, but they usually just sit and watch. They also forget they have kids on this day. The moms are Super Moms for the day—cooking and watching kids. This also happens every year.

We have our family favorites at Mom's: turkey, mashed potatoes, gravy, stuffing, corn, sweet potatoes, rolls, and pie. This menu will never change. Not only did we eat turkey, but we felt like a stuffed turkey!

So many dishes, pots, and pans. We have pots that need to soak. And we have scrubbing for the men. They have to help too! The day after, the men venture out for golf. I take Katie and Taylor to the movies. I wish Riley were going with us. Mom is going to rest before everyone comes back for turkey sandwiches. I always think a turkey sandwich is better than the Thanksgiving turkey! Aunt Donna made stuffed shells for dinner on Friday night.

Since we have so many out of town family, Thanksgiving is a whole weekend of eating, football, and catching up. We end our evenings with dessert and a movie. Everyone is so exhausted by the time they go home—especially Mom and Dad. They have outdone themselves once again!

Another year of wonderful Thanksgiving celebrations surrounded by people I love. I'm so thankful I have them. They've been absolutely amazing.

December 1, 1993

Taylor is getting so big! He lost his first tooth! The big teeth will soon be replacing the baby teeth. I guess this means he is not a baby anymore. When the tooth came out, he wanted to call everyone to tell them the news. He also reminded me about the Tooth Fairy. Brian and I had a huge responsibility; we had to make sure the Tooth Fairy was awake and had plenty of money!

Katie is trying to figure out Mary, Joseph, and baby Jesus. It really worries her than Jesus was born with animals. She kept asking: "But why, Momma?"

In the car today, Taylor said, "Mommy, God sent His Son to die on the cross, and the cross was made from a tree." He is right!

I really miss Riley this time of year. I wonder what he is doing and what he looks like. I wonder if he can see his earthly family. Sometimes, I look to the sky hoping God will show me a glimpse of Riley. I think I will always be hoping. I wonder if Brian does the same thing.

I am having an ornament made for our tree of Riley with angel wings. I am excited to put it on our tree. I am also having one made for Mom and for Carol, our friend who lost her daughter and helped me so much.

I think back to our first year without Riley, and I can see how far we have come. I can clearly see how God carried our family. I still have a bad day and still have moments of tears, but they are not too often. Life moves so fast, and sometimes thoughts of Riley appear. I suddenly want to go to Riley's Rock. I don't ever want to forget him. Sometimes, it can be so hard, but I am okay. The next day is always better than the last.

Good night, Riley!

December 11, 1993

Tonight while reading the Christmas story, I thought of Katie and Taylor. I pray we have not forgotten the true meaning of Christmas. It is so easy to think about presents, but this is about Jesus's birthday.

God gave us the very best present: His Son, Jesus Christ. Jesus grew up telling people about His Father. When His time on earth was finished, Jesus died on the cross for us. He did this so He could take away the sin in our lives. When I mess up, I have to ask God to forgive me and to help me turn away from my sin. Jesus is always waiting to forgive us. God wants us to have a happy life. He wants the best for us. God loves us so much!

Do you know why I love Christmas so much? It is because of Jesus's birthday that we will see Riley again! We will all be together in heaven one day. We all miss Riley so much, and there is not a day I do not think about him and how our life would be different with him here. Taylor would be the best big brother, and Katie would have that special twin bond. Bringing Riley to heaven was God's plan all along. God never makes mistakes, and one day, it will all make sense to our family. If we never experienced hurt or endured bad things, we would never seek or need God. Bad times bring us closer to God.

God, please help me to remember what the true meaning of Christmas is and to remind my children of it. No one can ever give us a gift like God has given us. All we have to do is receive the gift and then share it with others.

January 24, 1994

Bug has had another birthday and is now four years old! I cannot believe what a cutie she is!

When I asked what she wanted for her birthday, she said breakfast in bed. She is so funny! I cannot believe how fast she has grown up.

Mom and I took Katie and her friend Maggie to see Beethoven at the theater. Then we had a family party and invited Maggie and another friend, Michael. We also sang "Happy Birthday" and blew out a candle for Riley. Taylor helped remind us; he never forgets! Katie said she wanted Riley to sit next to her at the party. I know she knows Riley is safe with Jesus, but I wonder what she thinks about. We have tried to keep our explanations to her level, but we know as she gets older, we will have to explain more. Katie and Taylor always talk to each other about Riley, and I think it is so sweet!

I decided to write down some of Katie's favorite things at age four.

Q: What is your favorite thing to do?

A: Run errands with Mommy.

Q: Who are your best friends?

A: Kensley Partin, Maggie Matthews, and Michael Morris

Q: What are your favorite colors?

A: Pink and purple

Q: What are your favorite animals?

A: Barney and Baby Bop

Q: What things do you like to do for fun?

A: Singing, putting bows in Mommy's hair, getting her nails painted, wrestling with Daddy and Taylor. and teasing Quiggly, the dog.

Katie also loves makeup. She sneaks in and gets my makeup. She doesn't think I will notice the lipstick she has put on. Last week during a face check before school, I found one blue eye and one pink eye!

Today, we took the kids bike riding. Taylor is doing great on his new bike and will soon be able to ride without training wheels!

I love my family so much!

March 20, 1994

Today was the first day of spring, and it was gorgeous! We all went on a picnic on the Blue Ridge Parkway—even Quiggly! Brian led devotion on the Ten Commandments during our picnic. He is such a good daddy. He is so patient with the kids and wants to be with them at all times.

We went on a nature hike, and Taylor brought his magnifying glass. He found all kinds of bones. He is such a little scientist! We collected moss and brought it home to plant.

Taylor is growing up so fast. He signed up for baseball and will have to play with the big boys this year. He and Brian have been practicing throwing the baseball. He has such a great attitude and has such confidence. He is always happy and so easygoing. I never know if he is upset.

My dear friend, Diane Bouldin, died since I last wrote in my journal. Diane was so special, and I will never forget her. She had cancer, and in the end, the cancer won. When her hair started falling out, she called and wanted me to shave her head. I couldn't stop crying. I felt bad knowing this was the end. She was so positive and precious. I will never forget her smile and her sweet words.

When I got the call that Diane was being moved to hospice care, I had such an urgency to see her and say good-bye. By the time I got to her, she was unresponsive. Someone suggested Diane might recognize my voice. I went in her room to talk to her. I knew she was on her way to heaven. Diane squeezed my hand and said, "The first thing I am going to do when I get to heaven is give Riley a big hug from you." I was speechless. I told her thank you and that

I would never forget her. These were the last words I heard from Diane. Yet again, God gave me comfort and peace during a difficult situation.

Diane left behind her husband, Bill, and her son, John Noble. I will try to help with John as much as I can. Bill is such a strong man.

Diane made me a Christmas ornament. Every year, when I place it on my tree, I will remember her sweet spirit.

16

Several years after Aminal Factory, I found myself surrounded by activity: soccer, softball, cheerleading, church. When the kids were in school, I was working doing retail displays. But I started missing hairstyling.

I looked into taking the state boards for recertification. Even though I did my friends and family's hair pretty often, things had changed quite a bit since I was first licensed in 1984. I was so nervous to take the test. I studied constantly. I made flashcards and carried them with me wherever I went. I am dyslexic and learning comes more slowly to me. I spent a lot of hands-on time with my notes and flashcards. But I passed the test!

I rented a room in a salon in downtown Asheville. When the business closed, I found another space to lease elsewhere. Then *that* salon closed. I looked at many other salons, but they were all depressing and just not for me. So many doors closing! I had to look for an open door!

I announced to Brian that I was opening my own salon. It was going to be a place where clients were put first. No one works at the salon without understanding that simple rule.

When I opened my salon, I wanted the name to represent something good and pure—like Riley. I named my salon Riley's Salon Twenty One. I knew that name would always be a reminder to never lose focus of what the salon represented: a place for clients to feel better about themselves. A place where they are greeted with smiles and a hug. A place to relax. That is what keeps me on my toes working so many hours.

One of my customers from many years ago walked into the salon. She said she saw the name and knew it had to be me!

Whenever I get discouraged, it seems my clients know just how to help. Clients have let me know how much they love the salon. They knew it was different as soon as they walked in. It's a place they want to come.

Riley's Salon Twenty One *is* different. It is not my business but *God's* business. He continues to bless me in so many ways—not necessarily financially, but with clients who bless me every day.

So many times, sales reps tell me I need to make money. Or I need to do certain things to run a successful business. While I appreciate their advice, I want to let them know I have the best financial planner in the world. God has directed me from the day I opened my salon and has never let me down. I have never worried about the success of the salon. I prayed that if this business were God's will, he would only open doors for me. He did. I walked through and have never looked back!

The salon is my ministry. I pray that I stay focused on what is important and never lose sight of how important relationships with people are.

In a lot of ways, I feel hairstylists are like counselors. I take that role very seriously. Clients tell me things they may not share with anyone else. Not all clients are happy. But

I use this as a chance to encourage people. Many people save up money to get their hair done. Sitting in my chair gives them an opportunity to vent, talk, laugh, and share. We listen when the client wants to talk. We talk when they want to talk. Only 25 percent of what I do is about hair. The other 75 percent is about letting the client know I care.

I have met some incredible people in my line of work. When people open up to me, I am overwhelmed by their lives. A client I had never met before came into the salon and had such a sweet smile. She was beautiful. She let me know she was going through chemo and asked me to cut her hair. She was embarrassed to tell me she had a wig on. I asked her to come back the next morning so we could be alone.

Each time I am asked to do this, the reaction is always the same. Everyone thinks they are ready to see themselves with no hair, but the actual sight is so overwhelming. I have cried with so many women. It makes this ugly sickness real.

The next morning, when my new friend sat in my chair, she told me about her cancer. She told me about the day she found out. I could only say I was so sorry to hear this. In the midst of her trials, she was able to remain positive. She told me about her new grandbaby. Because she was so sick, she was away from work and was able to spend a lot of time with the baby. She continued to share with me all of the good things in her life.

I felt led to tell my story about Riley—how a baby who only lived six months gave me a path that I would have never known.

We had a wonderful time sharing stories and bragging about our kids. This lady had an incredible heart, and I want to be like her. I was supposed to be the one providing a service; she provided a blessing!

We have got to use our trials for good. You never know when you are touching someone's life and when someone needs what you have to say.

Dr. Norman Parks and his wife, Joan, were one the first couples my parents met when they moved from Ft. Lauderdale to North Carolina. Norm and Joan became a big part of our family. Dr. Parks was my pediatrician. He and Joan sang at my wedding. Once Brian and I started our family, Dr. Parks became Taylor, Riley, and Katie's pediatrician. He is such a special, kind, man with a gentle spirit.

Our families would get together often. Joan and Mom would get us together for parties, holidays, wedding showers, and baby showers. Norm and Joan's four children went to school with me and my brothers.

Dr. Parks and Joan were there for our family when Taylor got so sick in the hospital. When I had the twins, Joan and Norm were with us.

Joan was always looking out for the kids. Every time we got together, Joan would ask Norm to check one of the kids' ears, throats, or whatever else needed to be looked at.

The Parks gave us a red wagon just days before Riley died. They knew how much we loved to take walks as a family, and they gave us the red wagon, as a gift for the twins, that held all three children. When Joan and Norm gave us this special gift, we took a picture as a family with the kids in the wagon. We did not know that would be our last picture taken as a family of five.

In 2007, Joan had to have surgery. Our family was at the hospital to see sweet Joan before the surgery. When we came in, Taylor was favoring his foot, and she asked

Norm to look at it. She was always looking out for someone else—even when it was her turn to be taken care of. She was one of the funniest people I knew. Right up until the surgery, we were all laughing and cutting up. We said our good-byes and told Joan we would see her after the surgery. That was the last time we would see Joan alive. Joan did not make it through her surgery. The surgery was more serious than she let on. That was just like her; she didn't want anyone to fuss over her or worry about her.

She was such a wonderful mother, wife and friend. She will always have a special place in my heart. Not too soon after Joan died, my dad was diagnosed with mesothelioma. The doctor gave him three to six months to live. My dad was a fighter, but in the end, this awful sickness took his life. Norm was there with my dad in the end and was always encouraging him to pray with him.

Dad was the most talented man I knew. He could make anything. When I was a little girl, he called me Pumpkin. I'm not sure why, but it made me feel special. Dad was crazy about his grandkids too. He taught us all so much.

He taught me how to bait a hook, not something I wanted to learn at a young age; but if I was going to fish, I had to do it. As I got older, I learned how to take the fish off the hook with ease.

Dad is the reason I learned how to use specific tools for specific projects. While Dad was building a house, he became very sick. That didn't stop him. He had my brother Larry, my mom, and me helping. I even got to put on shingles! I loved it! I had my own tool belt, and away I went! I am thankful for those times.

Dad sure fought his sickness. Mom was with him through the tough road ahead. It was hard on her too.

Seeing her husband that at one time was tough and strong and then so weak and sick was devastating for her. It was very hard to watch Mom, little by little, doing what Dad couldn't do any more. She was exhausted.

When Dad's pride was gone due to him having to let go and let others help him, he gave up. It was so painful to see him this way. I remember two days before Dad died, he kept falling. We were all together at the lake house for Thanksgiving. When he took his last fall, I remember Katie yelling to God: "Why won't you take him?" I felt the same way. We were ready to let go and let him have peace.

When I looked in Dad's Bible after he died, he had a few cards and pictures from his grandkids. He loved them so much!

Before Dad died, he told Mom and I that Norman Parks would be a good husband for Mom when Dad died. He didn't want Mom to be alone. Dad knew Norm was a good, kind, godly man. We told Dad not even to talk like that. He was being silly. Dad died on November 30, 2009. I am sure he is spending his time telling Riley all about his big brother, Taylor, and his twin sister, Katie.

Wherever I go, I see my dad's handiwork. One of Dad's projects before he died was helping me get Riley's Salon ready to open. I had the vision; Mom knew how to make it all happen. It would then go from Mom's sketch to Dad's skill. I still have things to finish, but it has never been the same since Dad died. When a carpenter comes in the salon to do work for me, I always wish it were my dad. It still is hard even now. I catch myself thinking, *Would* Dad *do it that way?*

Dad gave it all he had to the very end. He would be at the salon with his oxygen tube attached. He was slower and had to sit and give orders. He loved to give orders! I think he kept a mental list, so when someone went by him, he would always ask them to get him something. He was simple and practical.

I will never forget the last time I cut Dad's hair at my salon. As I was cutting his hair, I knew this would be the last haircut I would ever give him. I wanted it to be perfect. I knew that this is the haircut he would have when he would meet Jesus face-to-face. I had to hold back the tears. I didn't want Dad to know that I even thought about his last haircut.

That's the thing about life. It keeps moving forward whether you like it or not. Mom and my sisters-in-law and I took turns doing Christmas at each other's houses. Then before Joan died, she and Mom took turns hosting. Usually, the Parks's and Adams's Christmas would take place the weekend before Christmas. The year Dad died, it was my turn to host Christmas at my house.

The Parks girls offered to host instead because they wanted to help after Dad's death. They are so kind. I did not want Mom to host. She was so lonely. Dad was all she ever knew. I wanted to have everyone at my house. It gave me something to take my mind off the sadness of losing my dad.

That Christmas was one we will never forget. Mom had come over to put a pork tenderloin in my oven earlier that morning. By midday, we couldn't smell the tenderloin cooking. That's when I heard my mom frantically calling from the kitchen, "Lori! Your oven isn't working!"

I panicked. Nothing was open, and our microwave could only cook so much. Christmas dinner that year was a big pot of Sloppy Joes. We still laugh about that to this day!

Here we were, sitting around a beautifully decorated table with gorgeous flowers, candles, and place settings eating Sloppy Joes! The dinner became a funny memory.

I remember looking at my mom and Norm laughing and smiling. Suddenly, a memory popped into my head—something my dad had told me before he died, "Norm would be a good husband for your mom."

17

As time went on, whispers were heard: "Wouldn't it be something if Norm and Carole end up together?"

They had the same couple friends, and when someone had a get-together or dinner party, it made sense for Norm to bring Mom. I think the first time they got together after Dad died, Norm asked Mom to go have coffee to see how she was doing. I am sure it was prompted by one of his daughters. Mom went, and the rest is history. Mom and Norm got married on 2010. It was such a special wedding.

Norm was so different from my dad. I think that made this easier for me and my brothers. Norm knew all of my family. "Papa" was with our family through the laughter and the tears. He always has a kind word, a smile, and will think about what you say and then give you the answer. He is patient and has a love for children and a heart of gold. His spiritual walk in Christ is real. He can tear up just thinking about what Jesus did for us. He has that love for God more than anyone I know. He loves me and my family like his own. Papa treats Mom like a princess. He spoils her. Mom deserves a man like Papa. She has always put others first, helped students with mission trips, and would give money to families in need.

One Christmas, we were at the lake house. Mom walked in the kitchen and said, "Lori, I want to give money to a family in need."

"Okay...what family?" I asked.

"We will just drive around and see if there is a family or person who looks like they could use some happiness," she said.

I was so excited! Katie was too and asked to join. The three of us took off.

We all had a mental picture of what we were hoping to find. We drove and drove and drove. We were getting a little discouraged because none of the houses we passed made one of us say, "That's it!"

We kept driving, and then all three of us saw a tiny house. There was wood in the yard for sale and a wood burning fire, and the house was falling apart. It looked like they had done the best they could. My favorite thing was the Christmas lights! They were strung all over the outside porch. It made it so special. Mom, Katie, and I were so excited but also nervous. What will these people think? Maybe they would be insulted and not want this gift.

We pulled up in the driveway, and a lady walked up to Mom's car. Mom said, "We have been blessed by God this year, and we wanted to bless you."

The lady started yelling, "Money for medicine? You are giving us money?"

She yelled for someone, and an older lady and many others came out of the tiny house. The first lady explained to the rest of her family that we had given her money for Christmas. They all jumped up and down. The older lady had tumors all over her face. She teared up and kissed Mom on the cheek and kept thanking us over and over. Mom, Katie, and I cried too. It was so special.

When we left, we looked back, and all of the family was in a circle holding hands. It was so beautiful. I don't think that we will ever know how bad they needed the money.

This is the kind of person my mom is! I hope I can be the woman that Mom is. I never take for granted what she has shown me and taught me. God has such a sense of humor. When Dad died, Mom was so lonely. God was in heaven thinking, "I have your mom in my hands. I will always take care of her."

God always fulfills His promises. If it isn't here on earth, it will be when we get to heaven. We have to trust Him. He truly knows what we need before we need it. After all, He created us. He is our Father who loves us with all of our mess, failures, and trash. I thank God for His grace and mercy!

God knew all along!

When I started writing in my journal twenty-three years ago, I never could have written a story like that. But God knew all along! God is so good!

Epilogue

When I started reading my first journal entry after Riley died, I had so many questions. I never knew I had been missing details in some parts of my life. As I read my journal entry from the morning I found Riley, I panicked.

"Who watched Taylor and Katie when I found Riley?"

"How did my neighbor know to come over?"

"Who found Brian when this all happened?"

"How did Brian go back to work so soon after Riley died?"

"What was that like for him?"

Brian and I went out for dinner a couple of weeks ago, and I asked him questions about the day Riley died and the months that followed. My life was just moving one day at a time. I was just trying to keep going. Brian said that he was so sad when Riley died, but he had to mask his feelings for me and the kids. He had to be strong for me.

I asked Brian how he went back to work so soon after Riley died. He said it was one of the hardest things he ever had to do. He went back, still not believing this happened to our family. He thought when he walked in the house after work, Riley would be there. His supervisors told him to take off more time. They couldn't believe he was back to work. Brian said he had to go back to work because we couldn't afford for him to stay out of work.

That hurt my heart. He was right, though. The coworkers at United Parcel Post were incredible. They collected money for our family. We are both so thankful to those men and women.

My mom told me that my neighbor was the one who watched Taylor and Katie. She saw the fire truck and police show up at our house, so she came to see what was going on and heard me screaming. She helped me get out of my pajamas and get some clothes on. I was too numb and in shock to realize what was going on then. Even now, I can't remember those events unfolding.

When I started writing my book, I got to look back with a clear mind and fill in the blanks of my past that I never knew needed to be filled in. When we go through the trials of our life, we cannot see the end results. We are hurting, mad, helpless, or bitter. It's only *after* we've come through them that we see how God was at work. By writing this book, I got to see God's work in the past twenty-four years. I had to put my trust in something unseen—a God whom I have believed in since I was seven.

As I went back through my journals, I started thinking about Taylor and Katie. I asked them how they felt about losing Riley and if they could write something for *Good night, Riley*. I let them know if they couldn't, I would understand. I said it could be a Bible verse, a word of encouragement for a mom, dad, or sibling—something that would be helpful for a parent to see from the siblings' point of view. What they gave me was amazing:

From Riley's Twin Sister, Katie Hauck

Twins. I cannot even imagine what thoughts went through my parents' head when they heard that simple word. The interesting thing about twins is that unlike other babies, when born, they get to share all of life's experiences with someone. The moment they take their first breath or their first Christmas, start preschool together, celebrate birthdays, walk into high school for the first time, go away to college. They have endless amounts of special moments with their closest friend. Riley was there for the moment I took my first breath. We were able to experience that first moment of looking our mom and dad in the eyes and recognizing the voices we heard while in our mom's womb. Riley was my twin brother.

God had bigger plans for Riley. He became our little angel shortly after being born. But the littlest of moments, I cherish with Riley. He was my closest connection in this new world, and suddenly, he was gone. Riley, yes, was taken from us at an early age. But our bond only grew stronger. My parents' strength never let Riley disappear. On my birthday, we would celebrate Riley's life by adding a candle or his name to the cake. We would send balloons up to him in heaven. Riley was never taken from me; instead, he is watching over me.

I remember laying in bed at night as a child saying my prayers to God and then asking God, "Can I talk to Riley now?" knowing he was sitting right next to God, watching as God took delight in me. My conversations were simple, telling him about my day or the friends I had made or the experiences I would go through. Riley was with me—even the moments that others felt he was "missing out on." I knew he was watching from above.

To this day, people ask me how many siblings I have. I always say two. Riley is not dead to me. I know he is in heaven, and because I committed my life to Jesus, I will see my brother again.

The moment that was the hardest to me, losing my brother, was seeing the hurt my mom and dad went through. During the time of his passing, I do not remember a whole lot of emotion; however, as I got older, I remember Mom having "Riley Days" or a blue day on the day he passed away. We would ask ourselves what Riley would be doing, what sports he would be involved in, what college he would attend, or what Riley would be doing now. My mom knows that Riley's story has truly been used for God's glory and for moms who have lost a child, but only through her strength in the Lord did she make it through.

I remember thinking to myself that while Riley was not able to live, I had been given an abundance of life. It did not seem fair to me. Throughout high school, my dad and I had a rough relationship, and I sometimes wondered if it was because he wanted Riley to have lived instead of me. This was never true, and my dad and I have the most incredible daddy-daughter relationship now.

God has plans for us all, and whether it be lifelong or only a few months, we all have purpose. I decided to have a personal relationship with the Lord in high school. High school was the hardest time for me, with girl drama, Internet bullying, and just plain mean girls. I was made fun of for my decision to follow Christ, and it was tough. I didn't understand at the time, but now, I am working with Young Life. My heart is full of love for middle and high school girls who are going through similar things that I went through in high school. I have been able to see girls come to know the Lord and follow His truths about themselves instead of mean things they may hear at school or at home. I know what they are going through and completely understand the hurt they feel. God has purpose for me.

*Riley was our angel. He did not live for very long,
but he is very much alive in our hearts. In my story
and in Riley's story, God is able to be glorified. That's
right. We can stand strong knowing God has a purpose
for both of us. I am so thankful for loving parents and
close family that has been given to me. We are memory
makers, and as my mom has always said, "We are not
rich in money, but we are rich in love." I wouldn't have
it any other way.*

From Riley's Big Brother, Taylor Johnson

*Losing a sibling is certainly a life-altering event.
However, when I try to remember the summer of 1990,
I have trouble recalling the events my mother wrote in
her journal. I am well aware of the profound impact
Riley has had on my entire family. But no matter how
hard I try, I truly am unable to remember that day.
I do have memories of Katie and Riley's crib and my
toys—most likely Fisher Price—in the den but nothing
specific from the time he was with us.*

*For most people, it's hard to miss something they
don't remember. The amazing thing is that while I may
not remember being around and seeing Riley myself, I
miss him dearly. The impact of a person, even an infant,
is incredible. It's been over twenty-four years, and I still
find myself asking if Riley would be proud of me.*

*My entire life, I have only seen the life of my brother
in pictures, home movies, and stories from my mother.
The idea of having a brother is almost surreal. Growing
up, I would (and still do) wonder what it would be like
if Riley were here—not instead of a sister, but what
things would be like with a family of five.*

*To some who have lost a loved one, their men-
tal picture of that person is the most recent memory.*

Some remember my brother as an infant, but because Riley was a twin, I am reminded of his birthday every year when we celebrate Katie's birthday. To me, he is a twenty-four-year-old young man. I wonder what sports he would like. Is he introverted like me? Or outgoing like his twin sister? I'm sure it didn't take long for him to realize Katie was a talker!

I ask questions because I know one day, we will get to meet him again. That's what I would encourage any brother or sister to remember. The loss of a sibling is never good-bye; it's "See you later, alligator." When I think about Riley, I don't get sad that he is gone. I get excited to tears that we will get to meet again. I've found myself teary-eyed and smiling at the same time when I've snuck out to Riley's Rock when visiting home. I don't even remember where it is in the old church cemetery, but just sitting at the base of the tree nearby is close enough.

If you are a sibling in my shoes, remember, you didn't say good-bye.

It was emotional for me to read what Taylor and Katie wrote, but that was one of the most meaningful parts of writing. For the first time, I got to experience their loss after all these years.

In 2012, my mom and I were out shopping one day when I heard someone call from behind me.

"Hi, Lori!"

It took me back a minute to place this woman because of my terrible memory. I replied and started engaging in small talk, hoping a bell or signal would go off in our conversation so I would know how I knew this woman. It finally clicked.

I remembered briefly seeing her working with students at a church I used to attend. What a relief that was! I now could have a normal conversation with Annette and not look like a forty-seven-year-old with dementia. I didn't know then, but God was bringing Annette back into my life for a reason.

Annette and I kept in touch here and there. And a year after running into her at a store, I started the path to write this book. As I began compiling everything I would need to write the book, I started to feel overwhelmed. I would start out with the best intentions and then end up getting frustrated and angry. I questioned why I was even trying to do this in the first place.

Then I would hear God's soft voice: "Lori, you're getting frustrated because it's an attack from Satan. He's trying to get in the way of my work. Don't give up. I've got a plan."

I pressed on. Late one night, I typed part of my journal, saved it, never found it. I did it all over again. This took me hours to do, and then I found the original saved in some crazy file. I tried to print all of the pages—just in case I lost it again. This would guarantee I would not make the same mistake twice. Then the printer stopped working. I threw my hands up in frustration.

"I am done with this!" I said to myself. "I can't do it! I am stupid, and I for sure don't want anyone to see this! I can't even type, save, or print anything!"

My confidence was at an all-time low. I had to walk away feeling discouraged and defeated.

I was reminded of Hebrews 12:1–2: Let us run with endurance the race that was set before us. Look to Jesus, the author and finisher of our faith.

I decided I'd keep going and see this to the finish line. But I also knew I needed help. Thankfully, God had it handled.

I can't remember where I was or what I was doing, but all I remember is God brought Annette to my mind. "Annette could help you with your book."

When this first popped in my mind, I thought Annette would think I was crazy. I barely knew her; how would I ask her to write my book? But all I could do is ask, right?

I finally got the courage to ask Annette if she would be able to help me out. I just needed my handwritten journals turned into a file to send to the publisher. I asked Annette if she wanted to meet for coffee. When we met up, I told her how God kept placing her on my mind to ask for assistance with my book.

Then Annette said, "I don't know if you know this, but I majored in journalism, and I used to be an editor."

I got chills, and the hair on my arms stood straight up!

Now I saw what God was doing. He took my weaknesses and put me with someone who was strong in those areas. That is why He brought us together. If we trust God in our life and trials, we listen to Him and act on it, God gives us just what we need at just the right time.

Satan did his job and added extra obstacles for me to overcome. I would say, "God, this is too hard! I don't know if I can keep going." But God always reminded me the purpose of this book. Somehow, I would be encouraged by a friend or a client and be given the strength for just one more day.

One of my sweet clients opened up to me about a miscarriage she had forty years ago. It touched my heart. Forty years ago and she still has such emotions after all this time. These are Donna's heartfelt words:

"We had always wanted a large family—four to six kids—so I was happy to be pregnant with my third. I was so excited! I already had a girl and a boy, so I had no expectations for the next one. I had easy pregnancies and deliveries with the first two. Life was perfect, and the more, the merrier! I knew my due date, April 23, and I was planning how I would add to the kids' rooms, depending on the gender, and I was trying to choose a name. I was doing the 'J' thing for first names, so James or Julie it would be.

"On a beautiful fall day, after apple picking at an orchard with the kids, I started having cramps and then started spotting. But I was sure nothing was wrong. Then the bleeding got heavier, and my obstetrician said I'd better come to the hospital. It turns out, I had lost the baby earlier that day—at about twelve weeks.

"No James. No Julie. No springtime birthday parties. I was devastated. My parents took my toddlers for a few days, and I grieved for my baby. I did not want to hear, 'It's for the best' or 'It was just not meant to be.' For me, it already was! I still think of that child every year on April 23; that was forty years ago."

To all of the mothers who have experienced the loss of a child, one day, you will meet that precious baby again. I think it is so comforting that I will see Riley again. When I gave my life to Jesus when I was seven, I had the childlike faith to accept the hope, peace, and comfort He offered. Because I am saved, I will see my son again. I have that promise, and it gives me hope.

What do people do when they have no hope? They just give up. Their life doesn't have purpose. They just exist and go from day to day. Don't you want your life to count? At your funeral, what will people say about you?

At my funeral, I want people to say I was kind and encouraging. I want people to say my life had purpose. That I helped others, encouraged others, and showed them that Jesus Christ can turn their messed up lives into something beautiful and full. I want them to say, "She was a woman of faith!"

I pray that as people read this book, they will find the One and Only way to a full life! He is truth and will give you peace as soon as you make Him the Lord of your life.

I am honored that God chose to reveal Himself to me. He chose to show me who He is and how I can see the good through the trials. I encourage you to ask God to show you the way, truth, and life. He is waiting for you to ask. God will not let you down—ever!

As I had the privilege to look back at my past, I got to see God's love firsthand. It took twenty-four years to see how God was taking care of me all along. If I did not have God to go to, my life would have been so different, and it wouldn't have been pretty!

When Taylor mentioned he was not sure what tree Riley is buried under, I realized the last time I visited Riley's grave with him, he was so little. We now have the picture of the tree above Riley's grave.

Brian and I went to Riley's Rock together and cleaned it off. We said a prayer and had a special time of reflection. We had not been to Riley's grave as a couple in years. We would each go when we felt the need, but we never went together. This was such a sweet time we shared as a couple, and it was such a time of healing. Our good friends went with us to take pictures of Riley's Rock and the tree he is buried beneath. We finally had a picture of the two of us visiting Riley's grave together.

A loss of a child can tear many couples apart. After twenty-four years, here we are—still together and closer than ever before! I love this man like I never have. If we did not trust God, whom do we depend on? Ourselves? No! That would have never worked. Brian couldn't help me through the loss, and I couldn't help him. We knew that if we were going to make it, we had to ask for God's help. He is always there to help us.

I never was into working in the yard. I would help Brian rake leaves and clean up the yard when needed, but other than that, I stayed away from the yard. When Riley died, so many friends gave us beautiful flowers. I planted every plant, tree, or bush. When I would have a bad day, I would go outside and work in my flower garden, and I would feel better. Digging in the ground, working up a sweat, and being out in the sun were refreshing. It was a good distraction from what was going on in my life. When I put my hands in the dirt and planted something, I felt happy.

I have heard a few people say the same thing. Gardening is such a distraction while grieving. When a new bloom comes up, it reminds me of Riley and of the special people who gave the plants to me. And gardening was a way to spend time outside with Katie and Taylor.

I would put Katie on a blanket in the garden to watch. She would scoot as close to the edge of her blanket as possible and test her limits. When she touched the grass, she immediately pulled back in surprise; she wanted nothing to do with life off her blanket. I picked her up and dipped her feet into the grass. Soon, she was walking and then running barefoot in the grass. She loved being outside.

Taylor loved to help dig holes in the dirt. He loved getting dirty! And he loved to get hosed off and play in the water. All that mattered to me was spending time with my kids. When Brian got home from work, he would join us in the garden. Taylor would follow Brian with his toy lawn mower. One day, I found him in his diaper and rain boots mowing with Brian. "Mommy, I'm helping Daddy!"

Children want to do what they see their parents doing. These are great teachable moments. We have to seize every opportunity. If we don't invest quality time with them when they are young, someone else will step in and do our teaching for us. This person could have a negative influence on our children. I never wanted to miss teaching my kids about the beauty of life and important life lessons.

Sometimes, like Katie on her blanket, we can be afraid to push ourselves out of our comfort zones. We have to be brave! Whenever I am scared, I try to think of Christ grabbing my hand and walking into that situation with me. When we trust God in the scary situations, we come out so much stronger on the other side. Baby steps turn into big steps: if you don't take the first one, you stay stuck! No one wants to be stuck in the dirt.

Buy a plant, get your hands in the dirt, and watch life grow. When it blooms, it blesses!

Some of you will read my story and question my God. All I ask of you is that you pray to see what He can do in your life. Your eyes will be opened for the first time. We all have our "stuff"—good, bad and ugly. God wants to take all of that and use it to bring us closer to Him. You may think your life is over or you are not worthy of a happy life. Yes, you are! Don't give up! God wants the best for you. God's grace is for every one of us.

The cross represents Him dying for you and me. He took all of our sin and guilt and the ugly parts of our lives and sacrificed His life for us! That is how much love He has for us. He died for us! Who does that! Jesus Christ does!

God is love. Keep your eyes focused on Him and not on man. God will take you to places you have never been before. He will bless you in ways you can never imagine. It is up to you. It is your choice to accept His love and grace or to ignore it.

Hebrews 4:16: Let us, therefore, come boldly to the throne of grace that we may obtain mercy and find grace to help in time of need.

From the bottom of my heart, I want to say that I love you. I pray for you. I pray you will find peace in reading my story.

To God be the glory!

Note from the Author

Riley's Red Wagons

The Riley's Red Wagon is a symbol that represents family-centered care provided at Riley Hospital for Children located in Indianapolis, Indiana. Red wagons are used at Riley Hospital to help families easily and conveniently navigate the hospital. Equally important, the wagons offer children a fun diversion from what can sometimes be a stressful time.

For a gift of $1,000, a "license plate" acknowledging your gift will be attached to the back of a wagon. You can choose whether a plate reading "Donated by…," "In honor of…," or "In memory of…" is placed on the wagon. As new wagons are purchased and placed into circulation, donors' plates will be used in the order in which gifts are received. Your plate stays with the wagon for the duration of its circulation at the hospital.

To make a donation and be recognized on a red wagon, make your check payable to Riley Children's Foundation, and in the memo line, designate "to Riley Red Wagon" and send to

Riley Children's Foundation
30 South Meridian St., Suite 200
Indianapolis, IN 46204

About Riley Children's Foundation

Contributions to Riley Children's Foundation ensure Riley physicians, researchers, and surgeons continue to provide the best possible care with state-of-the-art technology for seriously ill and injured children. Riley Hospital requires significant and broad-based financial support to sustain and expand groundbreaking, lifesaving treatment and research, and facilities and accessibility.

Riley Children's Foundation supports Riley Hospital for Children at Indiana University Health, Camp Riley, and the James Whitcomb Riley Museum Home. As Indiana's only comprehensive hospital dedicated exclusively to the care of children. Riley Hospital has provided compassionate care, support, and comfort to children and their families since 1924. Riley Hospital's partnership with Indiana University Health and its strong affiliation with the Indiana University School of Medicine make Riley Hospital a leader in pediatric care.

For more information, visit www.RileyKids.org or call 1-877-ToRiley (1-877-867-4539).

Lori's family (late 1960's)

Lori and Brian in middle school

High school sweethearts (Lori and Brian)

Lori and Brian's wedding (1984)

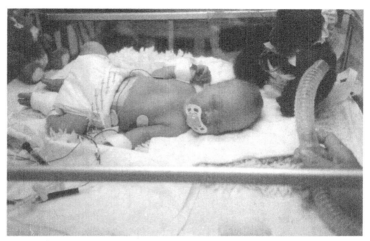

Taylor in the Neonatal Intensive Care Unit (NICU)

Taylor's first birthday

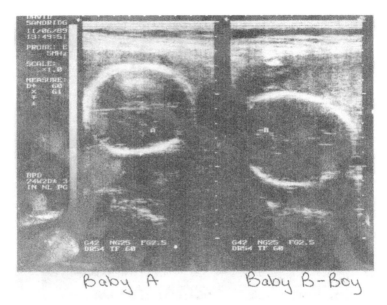

Baby A   Baby B - Boy

Ultrasound showing the twins, Katie and Riley

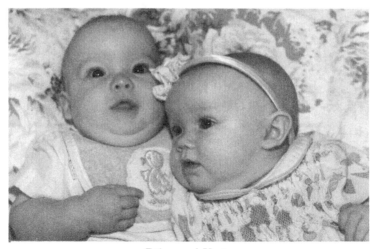

Riley and Katie

Katie and Riley's baptism on June 3, 1990 with Rev. Ed Graham

The red wagon from Norm and Joan
Parks as a gift for the baptism

Katie's first birthday

Picture drawn by Taylor of Riley as an angel

The gang at Halloween

Fall family portrait

Dr. Norman Parks

Picture drawn by Taylor of Lori at Riley's
Rock (Dirt and Flowers)

Kelly Harrison - One of heaven's angels

Riley's Rock

Lori and Brian at Riley's Rock 24 years later

Lori at Riley's Salon Twenty One

The family gathered for Katie's wedding

Balloons sent to Riley

Lori and Brian 2014

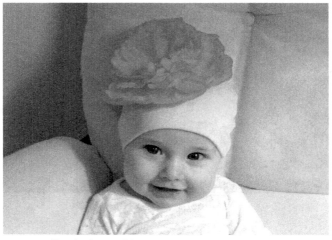

Selah Grace Hauck - the first grandchild

Two very proud grandparents

CPSIA information can be obtained at www.ICGtesting.com
Printed in the USA
LVOW04s1535220215

427891LV00030B/1132/P